The 24th

K E Hubbard

The 24th by K E Hubbard | Independently Published

© 2019 K E Hubbard

All rights reserved. No portion of this book may be reproduced in any form without permission from the publisher, except as permitted by U.S. copyright law.

This is a work of fiction. Names, characters, businesses, places, events, locales, and incidents are either the products of the author's imagination or used in a fictitious manner. Any resemblance to actual persons, living or dead, or actual events is purely coincidental.

ISBN: 9781081773380

For Grandpa Wilhelm, who taught me the value of a good joke and always asked me when my book was coming out.

Do They Know It's Christmas

Jack wasn't sure how long he'd sat in his cold car staring at a neon sign in the bar window, the only place open in his neighborhood at this late hour. He knew gulping down alcohol wasn't exactly a healthy remedy for his broken heart, but there was nowhere else to go except home to his empty apartment. It took all his willpower not to check his phone. Piper wasn't going to call. It was over.

He wrung his hands on the steering wheel and revisited memories of his relationship with her, deconstructing where it all went wrong, where he missed a sign or a signal that made it so easy for her to say goodbye. Her assignment was to profile a prince for her magazine. Not fall in love with the guy.

Reaching across the console, he popped open the glove compartment and retrieved the little black box he'd been hiding in there for some time. Prying the lid up, he ran his finger over the diamond, twisting it so he could catch a glimmer of light to make it sparkle. The moving speech he'd planned to give her while down on one knee had dissolved from his mind. Jack snapped the box shut and tossed it back in the compartment.

He dragged both hands down his face to reset himself. A little voice repeated in his head: *Go to her. Go to her, go to her, go to her.* He shook the nonsense out. It was clear Piper had no interest in seeing him, and he had even less of an interest in booking a last minute international flight.

He got the gumption to go inside and let a few shots of Jim Beam whisper devious lies in his ear. The dark interior hid him from the handful of patrons closing the place down, and he preferred that to anyone getting a good look at his face. He averted his attention from the couple flirting in the corner and the other slow dancing to a song playing on the jukebox. He plopped on a stool and flagged the bartender with a weak flick of his forefinger.

"Double shot of whiskey." Jack reconsidered his order, knowing it wouldn't be enough to drown his sorrows until they stopped struggling. "Actually, make that two."

A young woman beside him smiled behind the sheet of hair cascading over her profile. She absently stirred the ice in the bottom of her glass with her straw. He was surprised she even noticed him at all. No one ever did.

Jack adjusted the collar on his puffy navy colored vest and checked his phone for a missed call from Piper. His log was empty, of course. Piper was in Delbravia at the royal ball being twirled around the dance floor by the human embodiment of a Ken Doll. He imagined the way the prince kept his eyes only on her and wondered if she had completely forgotten about him, swept up in the dizzying passion of her so-called true love. He and Piper were average people, he thought, and average people didn't get endings like that.

The bartender dropped a pair of shot glasses in front of him. Jack pried his gaze from the woodgrain weaving through the bar top. The presence of the plush reindeer headband on the bartender's dome made him stuff a groan down deep in his throat. For the first time, he could relate to Ebenezer Scrooge's resentment of the holiday. Everyone was supposed to be cheerful and happy and sing the songs and be dazzled by the lights and all Jack wanted to do was wake up in January. Bah humbug.

He lifted his head and looked over his shoulder when the first stanza of Elvis crooning Blue Christmas came through the speakers. He massaged the tension headache in the center of his forehead. The woman next to him set her glass down and grumbled something under her breath.

"Do you ever feel like the whole world is conspiring against you?" she asked, her voice soft.

Jack sighed. He tossed the first shot down the hatch and liquid fire curled into his stomach. "It does today."

She eyed his drinks and folded the top of her straw into an accordion. "You look sad. Would it be nosy of me to ask you what happened?"

He started to reply, the words getting gummed up in his throat. It would be the first time he said it out loud. "I got dumped."

She hoisted her glass. "Hey, me too."

"I'm sorry. Worst timing ever, right?"

"Couldn't be better." She pushed her loose hair away from her face. She had eyes like a storm, and he was drawn in by their intensity. There was something else about her, something familiar, like they'd gone to school together or worked in the same building. He probed his already foggy brain for some context to place her in.

Jack's limbs grew warm and tingly. His inhibitions dropping in her company, he angled toward her. "How did yours end?"

A smile passed over her lips, and then it was gone. "He fell in love with the owner of the bed and breakfast he was staying in. They're getting married tomorrow."

"On Christmas Eve?"

She threw her hands up and let them fall into her lap. "That's what I said."

"I don't know if I can compete with that." The spicy aroma floated under his nose as he readied the second punishing shot. "My girlfriend was courted by the prince of some country I've never heard of. I was going to propose to her when she came back." He poured the whiskey onto his tongue to rinse the bad taste of saying that out of his mouth.

"Ouch." She spun her glass against the table, leaving a sweaty ring. "I should've gone upstate to be with Lincoln sooner, but I work so much it's hard to get away. I'm not sure if it would've made a difference."

Jack's vision softened around the edges, the multicolored bulbs in the windows bleeding together. They were one-upping each other in a misery contest not worth winning. "I read about Piper's love affair in the profile *she* wrote about him for a magazine. She didn't even have the decency to call me. I guess I was supposed to take the hint."

"Oof. That hurts." She extended her hand. "I'm Ella."

"Jack." He completed the handshake.

Ella ordered another drink, adding her glass to the graveyard of others in front of her. "What do you do, Jack?"

He considered where the night might lead if he opened his chest and let the heartache out to welcome Ella in. But he didn't want a fling. He wanted Piper.

"I own and operate a small chain of grocery stores," he replied. "What about you?"

"I'm a lawyer. I was settling the estate for my boyfriend's—*ex*-boyfriend's—family. His grandfather granted his advertising firm to Lincoln, but the will had a clause in it about his oldest grandson being married by Christmas in order to inherit the company."

It took Jack a moment to dissect what Ella said. "That seems unorthodox."

"Tell me about it." Ella's lips flattened. "If I'd have been there for the funeral like I was supposed to, none of this would've happened."

"Don't blame yourself." Jack almost put a supportive hand on her shoulder but stopped. He didn't know her. There was no need to cross the physical plane. "Your dude chose to be with someone else. On Christmas."

"Lincoln hates Christmas. He always said it was too commercialized." Ella drew a smiley face in the condensation on her glass. "He broke up with me in a parking lot wearing an ugly sweater."

Jack laughed, then covered it with his hand. Her seriousness evaporated and she laughed with him at the absurdity of it all. "What did he tell you?" he asked.

"He said he'd found someone special. *Special*," she repeated the word as if to give it another meaning. "Like I'm not."

The damning words in Piper's article flashed through Jack's mind. *On a sleigh ride through the farthest grounds of the Calvin Family estate, Prince Thomas of Delbravia's missing holiday spirit was revived through the magic of true love.* His head grew hot and itchy. He wanted to claw the thoughts of Piper out of there. A vindictive coil of jealousy wound around his ribs.

"We deserve better than this," he said.

"We do." She rested her chin on her hand. "A phone call at the very least."

"You should crash his wedding." Jack gulped. He hadn't meant for that fleeting thought to come out.

Ella's brows went up. "You know what? I should." She gazed unfocused at the line of liquor bottles on the back of the bar as her expression changed, a mischievous grin spreading across her face. "I can just imagine the look on his face when he sees me."

Jack put his elbow to the bar. "What would you say to him?"

Ella glanced at him, and for the fractional second their eyes met, that familiarity hit him a second time. How did he know her? It taxed his overcooked memory until she replied, "I'd tell him he doesn't get a happily ever after, after what he did to me."

From down the bar came a warning spoken in a husky voice, "I wouldn't do that if I were you."

Jack and Ella turned at the same time. A frail looking woman hunched over the far end of the bar, her skin stretched across crooked bones. She took a drag from her cigarette and blew the smoke at the ceiling.

"Why not?" Ella asked.

The woman tapped her ashes into a beer bottle. "Because you might not like what you find. When you upend the balance of matters of the heart, there are consequences."

Jack peered at her. "Sounds like you speak from experience."

"Oh, honey, do I ever." She swiveled in her seat. The modest red skirt flowing over her knees was capped by a white pinafore. She wore sensible khaki colored shoes lacking any kind of style. There was a twinkle in her cloudy blue eyes, something Jack recognized from his childhood.

"And you are…?" Ella asked.

"Name's Mrs. Claus—well, I *was* his missus. Kept the name after the divorce. I've got a new gig now. It's my job to keep jilted goofballs from getting into whatever shenanigans they intend to get into."

Ella laughed, open mouthed and loud. "Next you're going to tell me you have reindeer named Donner and Comet and Blitzen."

"I did," she said. "Nicholas got them in the divorce settlement."

Jack thought perhaps he was falling under the influence a little too quickly. Strange thing was, her act was convincing.

Mrs. Claus expelled the last of the soot from her lungs, followed by a wet cough. "See, you're stuck because you don't believe. And crashing that wedding isn't going to bring you any closer to what you really want."

"Well it's going to make me feel better," Ella said.

Mrs. Claus shook her head. "A temporary solution to a much

larger problem."

"Thanks for the unsolicited advice, but I think I got this." Ella rummaged through her wallet for a pair of tens, folding them in half and leaving them on the bar. "I hope your night goes better, Jack. Thanks for talking to me." She hung her coat on her arm and out the door she went.

Jack ordered a third shot and paid his tab, the buzz not working to temper his loneliness. The window framed Ella sitting on a bench on the curb alone. He should return to his apartment and start purging it of all reminders of Piper, but he rejected the concession. He was always there, like a human coat rack. Convenient. Handy and insignificant. Was he always this way? He couldn't think of an example of when he wasn't a footnote in someone else's story.

He waited a minute before he got to his feet, the slosh of alcohol heavy in his guts, and followed Ella for reasons he didn't yet understand.

"Careful," Mrs. Claus said, lighting another cigarette. "Things get messy when you disrupt the balance."

Jack ignored her and dashed out the door into the frigid jolt of December air.

Baby It's Cold Outside

Ella nestled deeper in her coat, big puffy snowflakes dusting her hair, and contemplated what to do next. To drive now was irresponsible, and it would take some time for the haze to fade. Her dramatic exit was a touch premature, and she kicked herself for not sticking around to talk to Jack a little longer. He'd gotten her attention the moment he graced the door, all shrunken back into himself like he was trying to become part of the scenery. It had only made her more interested.

She leaned forward for an unobstructed view of the street. There wasn't a pair of headlights, a pedestrian, or any public transit in sight. A golden glow from the streetlamps pooled on the sidewalk, amplifying how isolated she was.

She'd been there at Lincoln's side arranging the estate, certain she would be the one who would bring the settlement to its pre-planned conclusion. When packing his things for his trip, she'd found a ring box hidden in a zippered pouch in his suitcase. All through the ride to meet him she'd dreamed about how he'd ask her to marry him and where he'd stage it. She'd even practiced her surprised face—and it wasn't half bad.

Instead she stood there, mouth hanging open in shock at both his hideous reindeer sweater and his closing arguments.

Jack appeared through the dark, hands stuffed in his pockets. "Hey."

Ella's cheeks flared with heat. "Hi."

"Whatcha doin'?" He was tall and lean, the fringe of his black hair spraying out under his knit hat. The way he grinned and rocked back on his heels fit inside her memory, reminding her of someone, maybe an actor or a singer.

She fidgeted with the button on the pocket of her coat. "Waiting for a bus to come by so I could throw myself in front of it."

Jack craned his neck to look down the road. "You might be waiting a while." He sat on the end of the bench, putting the space of an entire person between them.

It became so quiet she could hear the snow landing on the ground at her feet. They glanced at each other and their gazes repelled just as quickly. She wished there was more substance to the moonlight to better highlight his features. And more time to observe them.

She slid a bit closer. "What are you doing tonight?"

His eyes dipped toward the phone hanging halfway out his pocket, then lifted. "Going home, making some food, watching TV maybe..." He peeked at his phone a second time.

She sensed Jack still harbored a ray of hope that would soon be smothered by this Piper person. Ella had been there herself, singing along to a song on the radio she'd never heard like the words were born into her. The car suddenly smelled of baked goods and she was bombarded by childhood memories that seemed manufactured, as if she'd lived another life.

"Come to the upstate with me," she said.

He smiled, and two shallow dimples formed in his cheeks. "Me? Why me?"

She smoothed a lock of hair away from her face. "If I'm going to a wedding, I need a date. And if I'm getting into shenanigans, I need an accomplice, and you seem like the right guy for that."

"I didn't think you were serious." He pointed over his shoulder with his thumb. "Are you worried about what she said in there?"

"Are you?" Ella couldn't say where this spark of rebellion had come from, but as a lawyer she didn't like being told no. Anything could be true if someone wanted it to be.

"The whole Mrs. Claus shtick did seem a little ridiculous. And I take offense at being called a jilted goofball." He blew a breath into his cupped hands and rubbed them together. "How long does it take to get to the upstate?"

Ella prodded her weary mind for the answer. The return trip felt effortless and quick in those winding country roads, like time was no longer a construct but bent to human will. "Five minutes? Five hours? I wasn't paying attention."

Jack nodded slowly. "That doesn't make sense."

"I was thinking about—" She cut herself off. "I was daydreaming."

He sat back against the bench. "I can't drive right now."

"Me either." She gawked at the cars in the lot, the windshields collecting thick coats of snow. She knew the higher elevation of the forests in the upstate would churn out even more of it, risking them getting stranded.

"Maybe we could…" Jack's eyes went wide at something behind her. "I don't believe it."

An engine shifted into a higher gear as a vehicle rounded the corner a few blocks away. A bus rumbled down the empty street, the brakes exhaling a long hiss when it stopped at the red light. The electric sign atop the windshield read UPSTATE in glowing letters.

Ella buckled her constitution. "Are we doing this?"

He clasped his hands between his knees. "Uh, I don't know."

"Say yes, Jack."

The light turned green. Her pulse ticked faster as the precious seconds slipped away. Without waiting for his reply, she dashed to her car and took her suitcase and laptop bag out of the trunk. She'd use it for her stay at the bed and breakfast after all.

"Come on." She hurried back as the bus parked by the curb. The doors opened and she hopped onto the lowest step. "Last chance."

Jack stood. "I'll probably go home and wait for Piper."

"She's not coming back." Ella pinched her lips together at Jack's wounded reaction.

He stared at his cognac colored boots and ground a toe against the concrete. His phone lit up the hollow cave of his pocket. The bluish glow enhanced the tightness in every angle of his face. She started to apologize, and he waved her off.

"You know…" his voice trailed. "Yes. I will go with you."

Jack helped her stow her suitcase and they separated to seats across the aisle from one another. The bus roared from the curb and any reservations she'd had were lost to the fog of gin and tonic. She would crush Lincoln's happiness and grind it to dust under the toe of her patent leather pump.

After a quiet stretch, Jack spoke again, "Piper's getting married. I can't believe it."

She pushed out a sigh. "I'm so sorry."

He removed his hat and scratched his head, tousling his hair until the front tips were all out of order. "I mean, she doesn't even know the guy. She met him, like, three weeks ago. How does that happen? Did I do something wrong?"

"You didn't do anything wrong." Ella reached across the aisle and rounded a hand over his forearm. He didn't retreat from her touch like she expected, and it made her feel more grounded too. "Nothing at all."

"She was the one. I always just knew." He slanted his gaze toward the window, and Ella was thankful she didn't have to see the hurt hiding there. "This'll be good for me. I can focus on something else instead of spending Christmas by myself."

It happened as she remembered on her last trek to the upstate. Sleigh bells jangling in the distance. A warm feeling pouring over her. A tiny flicker of unavoidable joy in her chest. Pine. What was it they said people smelled when they were having a stroke? Was it pine?

Jack rubbed his collarbone. "Do you feel weird right now or is it just me?"

Ella was relieved by Jack's companionship to help balance her. Since the breakup it was as if she was holding on for dear life to keep from falling off the earth. "I felt like this when I came here before. I think we're getting close."

The bus slowed at a ramshackle lean-to on the side of the road. It was as charming as it was useless. "Last stop of the night, kids," the driver said. "Hope you don't change your mind. Big snowstorm's supposed to come in soon."

"Still in?" she asked Jack.

"Still in," he said.

Ella was eager to escape the strangling air of the bus. Over the hill, Snowfall Inn waited under the gauzy glow of pearl colored strands of Christmas lights. The gazebo where she'd watched Lincoln propose to another woman stood like a mocking monument to her loss. Everyone gathered nearby was clapping for them. The audacity.

She couldn't deny it was a beautiful building, a two-story sprawling Victorian nestled in a backdrop of massive evergreens. A tree decorated in red and white ornaments filled the angled bay window. Greenery draped between the pillars supporting the deep front porch. The snowflakes drifting down like icy glitter gave it a magical quality.

Jack slowed on the walk to the entrance and tipped his head back. She wrapped her hand around the metal newel post at the bottom of the staircase and followed his gaze to the second level of the building, wondering if one of the windows was Lincoln's.

"Incredible," he said.

Ella couldn't stay still, itchy with impatience. "It's an okay building, I guess."

"No, the stars." He bent back farther, hands propped on his hips. "I've never seen so many."

She stepped into the place beyond where the light could reach and looked up. Thin wisps of clouds covered the blue-black sky, a billion points of light shimmering around the crescent moon. Jack traced a constellation.

"Orion," he said, inching into her space. "See the belt?"

The cadence of his words reminded her of someone else, but she couldn't pinpoint who. It made her heart stand up and pay attention. She closed her eyes to clear her wandering thoughts. They were there for a mission, and a rebound wasn't a wise decision.

They shook off the cold in the lobby and something about the way the snow flaked from her shoes seemed unnatural, too perfect. Ella approached the clerk, avoiding an errant glance into the adjoining den for fear of seeing Lincoln or his family. People in festive sweaters warmed themselves around a crackling fire in the fireplace.

"You're in luck," the cheery clerk said when Ella requested a room. "There's one more left."

The color left Jack's face. Ella cleared her throat. "I was actually hoping you had two. One for me, one for my friend here."

The clerk noticed Jack all at once as if he hadn't been standing there the whole time. "Sorry. We're all booked into the New Year. I could put you on a waiting list, but—"

"We're only staying tonight. We'll make it work." She looked at Jack. "Is that okay?"

He gave her a slight smile. "Sure." His voice was pinched.

"Breakfast is served at seven o'clock sharp." The clerk leaned into her elbow. "Our hot cocoa is the best in town. You don't want to miss it."

Ella took the room key, fatigue settling in. "I'm sure we won't," she said.

As they passed through the threshold toward the rooms, every head turned, and Ella and Jack froze. Lincoln and his fiancée weren't among the guests, but she scanned the faces twice to be sure. An older gentleman with rosy cheeks and wild white hair gestured to the doorframe above them. Mistletoe hung over their heads.

"Oh, we're not…" Jack began, redness flooding his cheeks.

"Yeah, I'm not…" Ella couldn't find a cogent response despite all the times she had to think on her feet in the courtroom.

Jack tried to explain. "This isn't—"

"Just kiss her already for goodness sake!" A woman gestured at the mistletoe with her coffee mug.

Ella grabbed Jack's wrist and dragged him through the room before either of them said something regrettable. She was so flustered it took three tries to get the key in the lock. She went in first and withheld a gasp, her suitcase tipping over and falling to the floor with a thud. Jack leaned around her and made a noise in his throat.

One bed dominated the center of the room, a canopy draping between the four posts jutting up from the frame. The crimson bedspread was decorated with lacy pillows. In the center of the bed were two pieces of chocolate in a clear bag tied with a big green bow. After the initial shock wore off, Jack flattened his palm against his chest and disintegrated into laughter. Ella couldn't help but join, covering her face with both hands.

"Still in?" she asked, cringing.

"I can sleep in the armchair," Jack offered.

"No, I will," Ella argued. "This is all my fault."

"I insist."

She looked at the bed, then at him. It wasn't fair to expect him to sacrifice his comfort after agreeing to travel all this way with her. "I suppose we could put a pillow barrier between us."

Jack considered it, rubbing the back of his neck. "It's sleeping. We don't have to make it a thing."

Ella nodded unconvincingly. "Exactly."

They avoided each other's eye. Jack picked at his cuticles. Ella collapsed the handle on her suitcase. Both of them tried to speak at the same time.

After a few pathetic attempts to move the conversation along, Ella finally excused herself to freshen up. She splashed cool water on her cheeks and washed her makeup off. The more the reality of what she was doing settled in, the more it amused her, and she smiled at her reflection.

She came out of the bathroom to find Jack stretched out on the left side of the bed eating a piece of chocolate. He wore a white undershirt, his clothes folded in a pile on the floor. A line of down pillows bisected the mattress. He breached the barrier and tapped the top of the bedspread.

"It's more comfortable than I expected," he said around a mouthful.

Ella slipped under the quilt and snuggled down until her head was the only thing exposed. She kept her hands tucked against her, so there was no chance she'd brush him by accident. She relaxed, the entropy of her overscheduled universe a distant thing.

Jack switched the light off. A few minutes later he was snoring. The weight of the silence kept her pinned to the bed. Though her body was exhausted, her thoughts wouldn't resign for the night. She wondered if this room was available because it was supposed to be hers.

That meant Lincoln was somewhere else—with his new fiancée. She balled the sheet in her fists. A tear she couldn't fight rolled down her cheek and plunked into her ear.

Her ruminations turned a shade darker. *A temporary solution to a much larger problem,* the strange woman in the bar had said. Guilt compounded inside her, making it hard to breathe. What was worse was that she'd roped Jack into her problems. He was vulnerable. She knew her advantage when she asked him to come.

"Jack?" she whispered.

He snorted and rolled to his side to face her, placing his arm on the pillow barricade. "Yeah?"

"Were you sleeping?"

He blinked slowly. "I was."

She held the bedspread to her chest like a child afraid of monsters under the bed. "Do you think I'm making a mistake by being here?"

"Did you change your mind?"

"I'm not sure." There was a catch in her inhale. "Maybe we should leave in the morning."

"How about we decide then?" He withdrew his arm.

"That's a good idea."

"Goodnight Ella," he said.

"Goodnight Jack." Her eyes fell closed. She reminded herself why she was here. As she sank into the arms of sleep, visions of Lincoln's miserable expression danced through her head.

Don We Now Our Gay Apparel

Jack snapped awake at a pounce on the bed.

"Wake up, sleepyhead!!" Ella exclaimed.

He pressed his fingertips into his forehead and coiled into the sheet. Last night's bad decisions were becoming this morning's regrets. "What time is it?" he croaked.

"Six fifty-five. I can't wait another minute." She flung the curtains open, the sunlight dull and low. She had a laptop and a workstation set up across the desk. Whatever lingering hesitations she'd had were long gone. "We've got a wedding to crash, so we need to fuel up and start strategizing."

Jack groaned and threw the quilt over his face. "I need five more minutes." As much as he wanted to reach her level of enthusiasm, he couldn't quite muster it yet.

It got quiet. Too quiet. Jack peeped out from behind his blanket barricade toward where Ella stood. He lifted his head. Like the bus driver had predicted, a storm had arrived overnight, draping everything in sparkling white mounds at least knee deep. He propped his chin on his fist and watched the flakes in their slow-motion freefall.

His attention drifted from the outside to Ella. Her long hair spilled across her shoulders and she toyed with the end of one of the locks. She was impeccably styled in a vanilla colored cable knit sweater and jeans, and in an unexpected detail, a pair of cherry red Chuck Taylors.

While she was occupied, Jack crept out of bed and into his pants and went to the bathroom. He braced himself before pressing the home button on his phone. The screen was blank. He hovered his thumb over the news alert he'd gotten at the bus stop about Piper's upcoming nuptial to the prince but kept himself from clicking the link. There was no sense reading what he already knew. His heart ached all over again, like a day old bruise reminding him of the injury.

He stripped out of his shirt and scrubbed his face and smeared Ella's toothpaste over his teeth with his finger. For Piper, he strove to be perfect, coiffed and flawless and accessible. He assessed his reflection, then ran water over his hands and through his hair, arranging it in the purposely unkempt way he liked to wear it when she wasn't around. His stubble was slightly overgrown, so he hunted for some amenities stashed in the drawers. Finding nothing, he opened the wardrobe in the attached dressing room and stepped backward in surprise.

"Ella! Check this out!" he called, cracking the door partway.

She appeared in the threshold and brought her fingers to her lips and looked anywhere but at him. He caught his own image in the mirror, the wide swath of his uncovered chest.

"Oh." He wrapped his arms around his trunk. "I don't... I wasn't... what am I doing?" He scrambled for his t-shirt and shrugged it on. It did nothing to hide the redness bleeding across his cheeks and down his neck.

Ella's eyes passed over him, then she removed the covering from her mouth. "You have very nice abs."

Jack flexed them under the fabric. "Thank you." With no graceful way to transition, he removed a green knit sweater from the wardrobe shelf and shook it out. "There's ten of these in here, at least. You're not getting something like this in a Marriott."

Her shoulders hitched with a chuckle, and he was thankful the awkwardness had subsided. "They're really committed to Christmas. Did you *see* all those people in the den yesterday?"

"Yeah. A whole room full of weirdos." Jack pulled down the sweater and spread his arms. The stitched white snowflakes danced across the front of his chest. "How do I look?"

"Appropriate," she said, following it with a sweet smile.

Jack's stomach lurched, that automatic reaction when his body knew something his mind wouldn't let him believe. He almost told her how pretty she was, but it seemed like he was toeing a dangerous line. He was there in a supporting role, where he was at his best.

They reconvened on the unmade bed, Ella opening a portfolio filled with handwritten notes unreadable from his position. "Here's what I'm thinking," she said, pointing to the top of her list. "First, breakfast. Most important meal of the day and a chance for us to get the lay of the land."

"And if we see Lincoln?" he asked.

She shrugged. "He's more of a black coffee for breakfast type. He was in and out of the kitchen every morning and straight to work. I can't remember him ever eating more than a muffin." She traced her finger down her paper to the next bullet point. "After that, we split up. I'll do a little recon to get some information, you interrupt the catering."

"Interrupt?" He couldn't tell if the sweater was too hot or his nerves were engaging in a hostile takeover.

"Disrupt, delay, cancel, whatever you have to do. If there's no dinner, it's hardly a reception." She grinned. "And you're the grocer, so I figured you'd have some insider knowledge."

Jack stroked his chin. The pressure to execute made him a little dizzy. He didn't want to let her down.

"After that, we'll go into town and see if we might locate the dress shop and the bakery. I wouldn't mind putting my fist through some fondant." She closed the portfolio. "Any questions?"

"Uh, no." He checked his phone as an excuse to dovetail into his next point. "I guess I need your number, in case we get separated or something. Or if there's an emergency."

Without a second thought, she programmed her number into his phone, and he called her, disconnecting when it completed. He couldn't help but be a little proud of himself for that smooth operation. Not that he was going to call her after this or anything.

They went downstairs and selected a table in the corner of the dining room away from the main entrance. Jack eavesdropped on conversations to pick up on anything useful. Ella had her head on a swivel. Without them asking, the host delivered two mugs to their table and boasted about their legendary hot cocoa. Jack would've preferred a hit of caffeine, but he wasn't inclined to complain.

Ella put her hands around the cup, steam rolling from the surface of her drink. "I need you to keep watch for Lincoln, just in case."

"How will I know it's him?" Jack asked, keeping his voice low.

"You'll know. He has wavy auburn hair and a beard trimmed so well it's like he stippled it on. His eyes are blue-green like ocean water. Great jawline. Warm laugh. Friendly smile." Ella drifted outside their conversation and into a private world of daydreams.

Jack took a sip of his cocoa to give his discomfort somewhere to go. The whipped cream melted in his mouth and for a moment it was the only thing he could think about. Suddenly he was reminded of the excited joy of Christmas morning. Waves of anchorless memories of times past filtered through his thoughts. Pine. Why did everything smell like pine?

"Drink your cocoa and tell me I'm not losing it," Jack said, breaking free of the trance. "Because this is the best thing I've ever tasted."

Ella quirked a brow, then took a sip. She swallowed and set the mug down. "Oh my goodness. That's…"

He didn't have words for it either. "Right?"

She tried to explain it again, "It's like…" She gestured at the tinsel and the decorations and even his sweater. "Right?"

"Right." He surveyed the room. The other guests were throwing their cocoa back like the shots he'd taken at the bar last night. They seemed a bit too eager, and Jack feared he was being lulled into complacency. He nudged his mug into the middle of the table, then hinged forward at the waist and whispered, "What's wrong with this place?"

"I was about to ask you the same question." She lifted her mug, then seemed to think better of it and set it down.

A sudden commotion to his right stole his attention. A man so handsome he could've come in with a halo strode through the door, received by unyielding adulation from the other guests. Jack tracked his effortless entrance into the room. The man threaded his fingers through his silky hair and seemed to lag a second behind reality as if he operated in a different dimension.

Ella knew. It registered in her entire body. "What's happening?"

"He's here," Jack replied.

"Oh no." She cowered lower in her seat. "Tell me everything."

Jack tried to act natural, putting his hand to the edge of his face and spying between the fan of his fingers. "People are congratulating him and shaking his hand. There was a really enthusiastic high five."

She curled her hands into fists and scowled. "A high five?"

Lincoln disappeared from sight, forcing Jack to do a casual turn to look over his shoulder. "Now he's in line for the breakfast buffet."

She kicked him under the table. "Go talk to him."

"Ow," Jack whined. He massaged his stinging shin. "Why?"

"To find out more about the wedding," she insisted through her clenched teeth.

"Don't leave me."

"I promise I won't." She nodded her chin toward Lincoln.

"Go."

Jack commanded every ounce of his courage and found his way between the tables to stand behind Lincoln. He rotated his plate in a circle, waiting for Lincoln to finish piling scrambled eggs on his. His collar irritated a ring against his throat. It took stepping into Lincoln's sight line for the man to make eye contact with him.

"Congratulations," Jack managed to squeak out.

"Thank you." Lincoln's smile didn't have a tooth out of alignment, his face symmetrical and his complexion dewy and unblemished, like he'd been created in a laboratory.

Jack transferred a couple sausage links to his plate, stepping sideways every time Lincoln did. "When's the big day?"

"Today, actually."

"That's great." Jack feigned interest, the niggling reminder of Piper coming back to haunt him. Couldn't she have waited at least another week to spare him the agony of being replaced? It was borderline cruel.

"The ceremony is at four at the chapel down the road and the reception is here immediately after," Lincoln said without being prompted. "If you aren't doing anything, you're welcome to come. The more the merrier."

"Cool." Panic grasped at him as they reached the end of the buffet line. He didn't know what else to ask. "I have a busy day planned. I'll see if I can fit it in the old schedule."

"You should go to the ice skating rink. It's fantastic." Lincoln's sea-blue eyes searched the room. "Are you here with someone special?"

Jack threw himself forward to block Lincoln's view of Ella. "I'm alone for the holidays. No one's with me, no one at all."

A look of offense came across Lincoln's chiseled face. "Alone? On Christmas? That's terrible."

"I just got out of a relationship. I'm taking some time for myself." Jack instinctively patted his pocket. He'd forgotten his phone in the room. In his negligence he may have missed the call from Piper, the call he hoped would include the words "*I was wrong*" and "*I'm sorry.*"

Lincoln clapped his strong paw around Jack's shoulder. "I found the love of my life here. I'm sure the same will happen for you when the time is right." He looked Jack up and down. "I like your sweater."

"Thanks, it's my favorite one." Jack's deep cringe didn't release until Lincoln removed his hand, the depression of his touch lingering after it was gone.

Jack returned to the table, Ella's chair bumped out and unoccupied. He sprinkled his eggs with salt and pepper but had no appetite. The tablecloth rose against his knees. Jack startled, shoving his chair backward.

"Well?" Ella whispered from under the table. "What did you find out?"

He kept his chin level. "What are you doing? I can't be seen talking to my crotch."

"Then get down here."

She yanked his hand and he melted down the chair when he was sure no one was looking. He settled the tablecloth as if it had never been disturbed and hoped no one would assume the table was available. Jovial laughter erupted from a group of nearby guests. In the chorus, Lincoln's full voice sang out a degree louder.

"Out with it." Ella folded her legs to her chest. She had a rogue flake of glitter on her eyebrow he wanted to brush away but didn't. Her hair fell in lazy curls around her shoulders, and he couldn't stop himself from thinking about raking his fingers through it.

He took a breath. The floorboards creaked. Jack kept his lips sealed until the person passed. "Ceremony's at four, reception here to follow."

Ella waited for him to continue. Her brows furrowed. "That's it? That's all he said?"

Jack raised his hands in surrender. "He was beautiful, and I got nervous. He's so *nice*."

She palmed her face. "Okay. That's all we need to establish a timeline. I'll sneak out the back and see who will give up information. You," she put a hand on his knee, "will work your magic on the catering. We'll rendezvous on the front porch in an hour."

He saluted her. Ella evacuated their hiding place, her steps placed with so much care they got lost in the noise of the room. Jack tented the tablecloth hem enough to see out. When he had a clear path, he army crawled into the dining room. Heavy footfalls clunked to his right and he didn't have time to react before Lincoln stepped on his back, popping the vertebrae between his shoulder blades. He held his breath and prayed for the sweet release of death.

Lincoln crouched at his side, the whoosh of motion wafting his cologne under Jack's nose. It had to be a crime to have so many perfect attributes. "You okay, buddy? Didn't see you there."

His mind spun a thousand different excuses. "No problem. I lost a contact lens." Jack walked his fingers across the carpet.

"I'll help you look."

When Lincoln's head was facing the opposite direction, Jack bolted for the front desk and asked where the reception was being prepared. The clerk was all too happy to divulge the details of the rental building at the rear of the inn. Halfway through her explanation, Jack quit listening, crunched under the constraints of time. A brief interlude of silence allowed him a chance to cut out of the conversation.

Once outside, the air filtered through the threads of his sweater and cooled his skin, making him shiver. A blanket of snow sat undisturbed and glimmering in the sunlight. It all seemed too sculpted to be real. He considered tromping through it to ruin its uniformity and imagined himself falling onto his back and cratering it with a snow angel.

He tapped his boots on the kickplate and stepped inside the party room. A dozen people flittered around tables assembling centerpieces and unfolding chairs. For the first time in his life, Jack hoped not to be noticed. His heart seized when a man carrying a bin of place settings made eye contact with him. Jack straightened and planned what he'd say, his word bank overdrawn.

The man set his box down and dabbed the perspiration from his forehead. "You must be the caterer."

"I am." His reply lacked any sort of authority.

"Let me show you the set-up." He hooked Jack's arm, escorting him deeper into the pre-wedding activity.

Jack kept a clear visual to the door in case he needed to make a run for it. "Did I already send you an invoice?"

"Right here." He produced a trifold sheet of paper from the pocket of his shirt.

Jack read over the order but took in no information. All he caught was the low guest count and the number of courses. A wedding cake wasn't included in the list. Ella may get her chance to destroy some fondant, he thought.

The man swept the random pieces and parts from the table, the ribbon clippings and broken leaves and other discarded claptrap. "I hope this will be enough space for you."

Jack delayed his response by giving the table a thorough assessment. "The space is great it's just—" Every head turned to him. He tugged his collar away and swallowed hard as he pieced together some jargon. "The snowstorm delayed my suppliers and unfortunately I won't get my deliveries in time to fulfil this order."

"Oh dear." The man put his hand to his cheek and shook his head. "That's awful news."

A woman wrapping paper tape around the stems of a bouquet came to them. "Are there any other suppliers?"

"It's Christmas Eve." Jack put his hands in his pockets, took them out again. "Most places are closed for the holiday. I wish there was something I could do."

Disappointment choked the room. He almost felt sorry for them, working so diligently for a last minute wedding—at least he would have if he was oblivious to what Lincoln did to Ella.

"Let me call and double check," Jack said, reaching for his phone. He stiffened when he realized it wasn't there. Everyone watched him flounder, and he received a few concerned looks in return. "I forgot my phone."

"You can use mine," the man said, taking out an ancient flip phone.

Jack thanked him and moved into an adjoining room to stay out of earshot. He dialed the number on the invoice and held his breath while it rang four times. Someone finally answered and Jack asked to cancel the order. There was silence on the line. He made up an excuse on the spot about Lincoln being stricken by a bad case of food poisoning. More silence. He could breathe again when they apologized for Lincoln's condition and granted the request.

When he hung up, he smiled at his success and punched the air a few times in celebration. To waste a few minutes making it seem as though he was exhausting all options, he called a few bogus numbers to add to the record. He relaxed his face to get rid of all traces of his excitement and walked back into the room with his head down.

"Unfortunately, there's nothing left for me to do. I'm really sorry," Jack said, handing the phone back to its owner.

There were audible groans. The man put his knuckles against the table and leaned his weight into them, the wrinkles in his face deepening as he pondered. "There won't be food for the guests."

"Poor Abby," the woman said. "She'll be so disappointed."

Jack tucked that name away for later. "Yeah it's a real bummer," he said.

She set the roses in a vase and stared at him, eyes pleading. "We can't let them down."

The man lit up, his brows lifting. "I've got leftover cookies from our decorating party. With my family in town, we'll have extra hands to get more made and frosted."

"And I can whip up a few casseroles," another woman said. "They're my specialty."

The little snowball of a suggestion became an avalanche. Others in the room offered to cook and bake and prepare and Jack found himself getting closed out of the circle. Every time he tried to add a comment he was drowned out by another helpful idea. As the group brainstormed how to save Lincoln and Abby's reception, Jack receded toward the door and escaped to the outside.

He grumbled to himself as he plodded along and contemplated how to salvage his failure. He wondered why everyone was so invested in a relationship between two people they didn't know. The fact that the wedding was so sudden didn't seem to raise any suspicions either.

He returned to the room and found his phone where he'd left it on the bathroom counter, steeling before he checked it. He counted backward from three and let his fingertip fall. The screen showed the time and date and nothing else.

Jack landed on the lip of the bathtub like his knees had gotten whacked from behind. His stomach roiled and sweat broke out on the back of his neck as if he was running a low grade fever. He scrolled mindlessly through his photo album to further punish himself. There was one of Piper in a cute hat with a fuzzy ball on top. Their disembodied hands clinking lattes together. Her laughing while untangling a ball of lights. He scrolled and scrolled until he hit the end of the archives. For the first time, something stood out to him, poking him in the eyes.

Their photos together stopped somewhere around mid-

December. He swiped his thumb over the screen but there were no more stored in his app. What struck him even more was the repetition. No seasons other than winter. No green leaves. No attire aside from sweaters and boots.

Jack blinked to reset his vision. They'd been dating since last Christmas. He knew that with absolute certainty. Why hadn't they captured any memories in between? Had he erased them by accident? He checked his deleted photos file. Empty. Another fissure crackled through his heart.

In a daze, he staggered out of the bathroom and into the harsh bite of cigarette smoke. Mrs. Claus fanned her hand near the open window to dissipate her gray exhale.

He screamed and clutched his thudding heart. "What are you doing here? How did you get in my room?"

"Go home, Jack," she said, a picture of calm. "There's a bus arriving in a half hour."

He peered at her. "Why?"

She pushed off the windowsill and approached him, a more intimidating move than he expected. He backed away. "It's for your own good," she said.

Everyone was always shepherding him around. Stand here. Get out of the way. Take my picture. *Didn't see you there.*

"No." He squared his shoulders. "I told Ella I would come. I'm not bailing on her now."

Mrs. Claus stuck an unlit cigarette in her mouth, the stick flapping in rhythm with her words. "Remember what I said about the balance?"

Jack didn't remember, nor did he care. He jammed his phone

in his pocket. "I've got to go."

"There will be consequences!" she called behind him.

He sped away from her and out the door. A snowball pegged him in the face, a wet cold blast. Another line drive chipped his arm. Ella popped out from behind the fender of an SUV, grinning like a fiend. The gentle sunshine forking through the trees cast her in a soft glow.

He scooped up a handful of snow from the railing and lobbed it at her. It missed by a mile. "I wasn't prepared for battle! That violates the rules of engagement."

"I make my own rules." She spun a set of car keys around her finger. "I got us a sweet ride. Hurry up!"

"How did you get a car?" He descended the stairs to join her.

"I asked the desk clerk for directions to town and she just gave me hers. These people don't have great judgement."

Ella started the car and it took a moment for the temperature to become tolerable. "How did it go?"

Ashamed, Jack turned to her. "I canceled the catering, but everyone started volunteering to bring food and it got out of hand. The food and dessert are still a go."

Her shoulders sank.

"I'm really sorry."

"That's all right." She shifted into reverse. "It was a good effort, and I have some information we can use to our advantage."

He wrestled with telling Ella about his encounter with Mrs. Claus, but he didn't want to curb her determination, so he kept it to himself. Maybe the balance needed disturbed, shaken up like a snow globe so the details fell more in their favor.

Marshmallow World

Jack didn't have much to say in the short commute to town. Ella wanted to tug on one of his frayed ends to unravel what he kept so neatly sewn together. His lack of conversation left a gap she filled in with reflections on her time with Lincoln. The man she'd seen in the dining room was not the same person she dated. There was a softness to him when he'd spoken to Jack, and he'd smiled more in their brief exchange then he ever did at Ella.

Ella had managed to learn his fiancée's name through a friend who was putting signage up at the end of the driveway. According to the friend, Abby had been doing bookkeeping for Snowfall Inn that morning to make sure all the financials for the rest of the year were handled before the wedding. If Ella didn't loathe her, she'd commend her for being so efficient.

She'd managed to con Abby's friend into giving her the names of the dress boutique where Abby was scheduled for final fittings and the jewelry store where Lincoln planned to buy rings. It would require her and Jack to split up again, which she regretted, because he seemed like a lonely soul. If they managed their time properly, they could reserve a few hours for activities that didn't involve weddings or Lincoln or Abby.

They rolled into town, which was so quaint and pristine it could've been a painting. Small shops lined the main road, their frosty windows decorated with paper snowflakes. People spun and slid and tumbled on the outdoor ice skating rink. Even with the car windows sealed she could hear the excited shrieks of children. The idyllic setting wouldn't be complete without a gazebo. So many gazebos in this godforsaken place.

"What's your plan?" Jack seemed sad or sorry, but she wasn't sure which.

She found a parking spot right in the center of the action—a feat she'd never achieve in the city—and switched the car off. "I found out where they'll be shopping for attire and rings. Rumor has it they're together here somewhere picking up gifts for the bridal party."

He became consumed by something on his phone screen, and that was where his attention stayed. His eyes were duller than before, even in the bright sunlight.

"Important business?" she asked, trying to put a lighthearted lilt at the end of her question so he knew she wasn't being serious.

He clicked his screen off and stared into its blackness. "Nah."

Ella searched Jack's face, hoping she could coax him into eye contact with her. "Are you okay?"

"Yeah. I'm good." He produced a smile, but his dimples didn't appear.

Jack didn't know that while he was sleeping, she'd spent some time looking for the article Piper had written about the notorious bachelor prince of the country he'd never heard of. In language so saccharine it could've given her a cavity, Piper described their love, how they "just knew" they were right for each other. The photo accompanying the article showed a beaming, doe-eyed Piper gazing lovingly at him. Ella had to close her computer to end the torture of reading it.

She glanced sideways at Jack, with his messy hair and his snowflake sweater and his shy demeanor. She'd take Jack any day over Prince Blah Blah Blah of Who Cares.

They immersed themselves in the crowded shopping area. She caught herself evaluating the passersby in their similar attire and almost identical expressions of open-mouthed wonder. Carolers filled the air with song. Bells chimed. Romance blossomed everywhere, and she was beginning to feel like an extra in a rom-com.

Jack kept his chin down but his eyes alert. "You ever notice we don't look like anybody here?"

"It's like you read my mind," she said, stepping around the slush to keep her shoes dry. "It's all a bit homogenous."

The farther Ella wandered into town, the more she felt lost in a Christmas labyrinth. If she got too deep, she may never see her way out. She considered taking Jack's hand so they blended better with the endless coupling around them, but his rigidness convinced her otherwise.

Santa's workshop was a flurry of activity, a line of children curling around the building. The ends of Saint Nick's velvety jacket overflowed the arms of his throne, and for a moment she believed he truly was that woman's ex-husband, if the whole notion wasn't so preposterous.

Jack nodded toward it. "Want to go tell him what you want for Christmas?"

"I'm not sure if Santa delivers revenge," Ella replied, souring at the reminder of the whiplash of emotions she experienced when Lincoln ended their relationship.

"What kind of package do you think that comes in?"

"A dish served cold."

Jack adjusted his collar. "Remind me to stay on your good side."

"Wouldn't you want to do the same to Piper? To make her feel as bad as she made you feel?" She found it easy to be frank with Jack, as if they'd had a lifelong friendship.

He gnawed on the inside of his lip. "I loved Piper."

"And I loved Lincoln. But that doesn't mean I should forgive him."

"It was different with us." Jack grimaced at his admission, and she wondered what the distinction was between his circumstances and hers. Their stories were the same, minus the royalty. He covered for his blunder and said, "I thought it was, anyway."

Before she could present a counterargument, a woman floated past her line of vision like a slowed reel, and Ella knew right away who she was. The diamond ring on Abby's hand spread the sunlight into a colorful prism. Ella whipped around and hugged Jack around the middle, using his torso as a buffer. He kept his elbows elevated from his sides like he'd become an ice sculpture.

"I saw her," Ella whispered into his shoulder.

"*Her*, her?" The subtle upward shift in his chest felt enormous against her as he scanned the distance. She didn't regret catching an accidental eyeful of him shirtless this morning.

She rotated him like a periscope. "She went that way."

Jack relaxed against her, warm and soft. "The one in the tan coat?"

"That's her." Ella's jealousy was boiling over in the form of frustration. She needed to keep a level head and not give in to it.

He leaned to the side, and she moved along with him. "She went into the dress shop." As she was about to release him, he gasped and held her closer. She breathed in the scent of his laundry detergent and it took her mind off what he said next. "I see Lincoln too. He's headed up the block."

Ella broke contact but wouldn't have minded spending a little more time pressed up against him. She couldn't determine if the heat in her face was from the cold wind or from his closeness. "You follow Lincoln, I'll do some sabotaging of her dress choice. We'll meet at the skating rink in forty-five minutes."

Jack read the time on his phone. "What am I supposed to make Lincoln do?"

"The opposite of whatever he's trying to do."

He puckered his lip. "I really wish I had gone to law school."

Ella laughed. "It's helpful in many circumstances."

They parted ways toward their targets. A few steps later, Jack looked back at her at the same time she looked back at him. It was significant and jarring and wonderful all at once. She almost ran to him and asked him to forget everything they came for.

But she couldn't when there was work to be done.

Ella inspected Abby through the window, wondering what it was that had stolen Lincoln's heart in such a short time. Abby's complexion was pinker than Ella's. Her pin-straight hair fell across her shoulders just so, a little breeze fluttering her bangs from her face. When she disappeared behind a curtain, Ella made her move.

A seamstress approached, but Ella declined her assistance, drawing out dresses and pretending to be interested in their intricacies. She had no plan, no exit strategy, nothing but blind rage guiding every decision. She slowed her thoughts and managed each one carefully.

An exclamation from the seamstress ripped her gaze up. Abby silenced the shop with her reveal.

"Oh, Abby. You're breathtaking," one of her helpers said, both hands crossed on her chest.

The simple gown complemented Abby's every curve, intricate stitching on the bodice reinforcing its elegance. Lacy sleeves elongated her already lithe arms. Ella was mesmerized, too afraid to rock the delicate balance of the universe with a clunky movement.

The acute wound of Lincoln's infidelity woke her from her catatonic state. As the helpers circled around Abby, taking a nip here and a tuck there, Ella meandered to an unattended pair of scissors on the table nearby. A slash and shred and snip and that dress would be toast.

She put the scissors back, reframing her vindictive intentions. If she wanted to be successful, she needed to take a different tack. The best way to sway someone was to plant doubts, then capitalize on them. Ella breezed through the dress displays, maintaining the act.

The women assisting Abby left her to admire her reflection. Abby gathered her hands at her waist and mimed holding a bouquet. Ella seized on the opportunity.

"You look beautiful," Ella said, biting her tongue as reminder to mask her contempt.

"Thank you." Abby stood sideways and reviewed her profile.

Ella tapped a finger on her lips. "But the dress isn't right for you." The comment neutralized Abby's excitement.

"It isn't?" she asked, brow furrowing with sincere worry. "What's wrong with it?"

She put a hand on her hip. "It's so plain. Shouldn't you go bolder on your wedding day?"

"Well—"

"You need a dress that makes a splash when you enter. I'm talking taffeta, I'm talking lace, I'm talking crinolines." She slid dresses down the rack until she found one matching her description. "You need a dress like this."

Ella whipped the behemoth of a dress out in front of her, the skirt so full and wide it could've been used as a sail. The sleeves were puffed up like valences, the bodice glittering with thousands of sequins.

Abby sucked her teeth, then forced a polite smile. "I'm not sure if that's my style."

"Of course it is!" Ella lugged the thing toward Abby's riser and hung it on the hook. She was surprised the hanger didn't plead for mercy under its weight. "In this dress, you'll look like a princess, like the woman marrying the prince of Del—Delbrovenzia or whatever that country is called."

"I don't know about that." Abby strummed her fingertips down the bodice.

A seamstress came to Abby's rescue. She propped her cheaters on top of her head. "Who might you be?"

"A visitor to your lovely town. I've been working for a prominent designer in Milan and needed to get away. Your shop has such a broad selection for inspiration." Ella fluffed the skirts and its miles of fabric. "I've worked with all the greats."

She crossed her arms. "Which ones?"

Ella hummed and not a single name came to her. Her lie had become too specific. "Most of them."

Abby's lip curled as she considered the dress. "I thought simple was best, but maybe I should listen to a designer from Milan."

The seamstress' brow went up. "I suppose." She wasn't convinced, but that didn't matter. Doubt had taken root. It was time to irrigate it.

"What do you think would command your fiancé's attention? What would knock him over in shock when he saw you?" Ella asked, picturing anyone but Lincoln in her mind.

Abby steepled her fingers, then laced them together. "We haven't talked about that. With all the planning it hasn't come up."

Ella worked her jaw. "How long have you been engaged?"

"A few days."

"I see." Ella undid the bustle and stretched the train across the floor. "And when are you getting married?"

"Tonight."

Ella took a breath before straightening. It was one thing to know the detail, quite another to hear it spoken aloud. Unexpected tears pressed against her eyelids. She found a kernel of courage deep inside herself to continue. "Try it on. You may change your mind." Just like Lincoln did.

The seamstress shot Ella a skeptical glance when Abby agreed to be fitted in a dress so wide it almost didn't fit through the doorway. While they were occupied, Ella texted Jack for an update.

He replied: *The target is in my sights. Preparing for a take down.*

Silver and Gold

Jack couldn't touch the jewelry display case for fear of leaving a sweaty handprint on the glass. He hadn't been able to salvage the catering fiasco and he didn't want to repeat his mistakes. This time, he'd do it with gusto.

He'd been stalking Lincoln from the tuxedo shop to the bakery to the jewelry store, ducking into crowds and once joining in a family photo to avoid being seen. Lincoln had spent no more than a few minutes at the first two shops, but it seemed he was planning on spending the rest of his afternoon browsing rings. He had three different bands lined up in front of him, taking his sweet time holding each up for inspection. Jack refused help from the employees, snaking his way to where Lincoln stood until they were almost shoulder to shoulder.

Lincoln glanced up and did a double take. "Hey! Sweater guy."

"Yeah, hi." Jack squirmed at the nickname. It was on par with "buddy."

He turned his wrist to examine the other side of the ring as if it wouldn't be exactly the same on both sides. "Last minute shopping?"

"I need a gift for my mom."

Lincoln looked from the display to Jack and back at the display again. "You're buying your mom an engagement ring?"

Jack swallowed hard. He passed the error off with a laugh. "That's embarrassing. I don't really know my way around a jewelry store, I guess."

A smirk livened Lincoln's face. "I know how hectic the holidays can be. Messes with the mind."

Jack almost skulked away in shame but decided to position himself at the case like he belonged there. No retreat. No surrender. A memory flashed through his mind of the day he picked up Piper's ring from the jeweler. She'd left him more than a few hints, dogeared corners in magazines, cutouts tacked to the vision board in her office. When her editor had to cancel the Delbravia trip at the last second, Piper volunteered to go in her place, and Jack was happy to see her pursue an opportunity guaranteed to earn her a promotion. It gave him a few weeks' time to plan every part of the engagement that never was.

After several unbearable minutes of pondering, Lincoln asked, "Could I get your opinion on something?"

"Of course." Jack tried to imitate the unearned confidence in Lincoln's posture, but it only made him feel more obtuse, as if he wasn't in command of his own body.

'What do you think about this ring?" Lincoln unfurled his hand.

To Jack, it was identical to the other two. If anything, they were boring. "It's nice," he said.

Lincoln nudged his hand forward as if Jack hadn't looked closely enough. "What do you like about it?"

"It's, uh," Jack scratched his head hoping to loosen an answer, "it's white gold and it's round. What more could you ask for in a ring?"

Lincoln slipped it on his finger. It rested above his knuckle. "I just want everything to be perfect."

He'd hoped for that too, designing the setting and the mood and the passionate words of his proposal to show her what she meant to him. He had been as self-assured as Lincoln in the days leading up to her return from Delbravia, ready to set foot into the future with her. Then, in a three-page essay, he'd learned her true feelings about him.

Jack projected those unsettled emotions onto the man still debating over a ring. "Getting nervous?" he asked.

"A little." Lincoln rearranged the rings as if by order of priority.

He folded his arms and put his back against the display. "I suppose that's normal when you make emotional, impulsive decisions that have lifelong implications." Where did that improvisation come from? He sounded like a therapist.

A jeweler came to assist Lincoln, and after a few arguments with himself, he selected an unremarkable band from his collection. "When I met Abby, I knew she was the one. I don't have any doubts."

"How long have you been together?" Asking the question made Jack's teeth itch.

"We met at the beginning of December and fell in love right away. I've never been more certain of anything in my life. The problem is, I had a—" Lincoln stopped himself, and the crack showed through his impeccable façade. Jack thought of Ella muffling her cries in the dark last night, agonizing over the mistake she assumed she was making. He went on, "There were some obstacles at first. But it all worked out."

"Seems like it." Jack convinced himself he'd sensed a vibration from his phone. It gave his idle hands something to do.

Lincoln looked at him for a long time. "Do you think I'm moving too fast?"

Jack lifted his gaze. Lincoln didn't want honesty. He wanted one-sided reassurance Jack wasn't going to bestow on him. "A few weeks isn't a long time to get to know someone, let alone marry them."

Lincoln rubbed his square jaw. "Maybe."

"You should talk to Abby about it. Really be sure."

"You're right." He nodded. "You're absolutely right. I should go talk to her."

Goosebumps branched out across Jack's arms. "I didn't mean—"

"Thanks for the advice." Lincoln collected his purchases and went for the door with a spring in his step.

Jack wasn't fast enough to catch him. "Wait!" he called. "Not *now*." People filled in around him on the sidewalk. He shaded his eyes with his hand and searched for Lincoln but couldn't pick him out from the others.

As if the floodgates had been let out somewhere down the way, the walk became jammed with people. Jack threaded the wrong direction through the throng, people crashing into his side and stepping on his toes. He squeezed between narrow openings and forced his way forward. He took his chance at a break in the crowd only to be intercepted by a choir of carolers.

He was blocked in every direction. People wandered closer to listen to the carolers sing. Stuck in the center of the audience, there was nowhere for him to go. He crossed his hands at his waist and propped a smile on his lips as the carolers reached the end of the first verse of "Joy to the World."

Jack tried to start the applause and they went into the second verse. And the third. Jack didn't remember the carol being so long.

With his options to intercede dwindling, Jack sent Ella an SOS. He waited for a response. It didn't come.

Across the distance, he spotted their meeting place, the slick sheen of etched ice reflecting the sunlight. He checked the time. Five minutes to spare. The crowd applauded the carolers and Jack muscled his way out and ran for his destination, weaving through clusters of people and almost clobbering a child toddling along with a stuffed snowman. He sprinted to the ice rink and made several laps around the perimeter looking for Ella. He called her. No answer.

Jack's jaw dropped when he saw Lincoln, his stride brisk as he made a beeline for the dress shop. An idea popped in his head, so outrageous it might work. He sent a message to Ella regarding his intentions and rushed to the skate rental shop.

He paid for a pair of skates and hurried to lace them tight. "I need you to make an announcement," he said to the kid at the counter.

His eyes narrowed. "Uh, what do you want me to say?"

Jack gripped a support post to stabilize himself. "I'm about to attempt something I've never done, and I'm probably going to hurt myself doing it, but I want everyone to look at me."

And with that, he stepped across the entrance and onto the ice.

Do You Hear What I Hear

Abby's frown deepened as she stared at herself in the mirror. The dress was like a melted candle, big blobs of taffeta pooling all the way off her riser and touching the floor. She was swallowed up by the marshmallow fluff shoulder pads. Every attempt she made to use her posture to overcome its obnoxious size was futile.

"That's it," Ella said, putting both hands together and cackling internally. "That's the dress."

The seamstress sent her a disapproving glance. She moved her glasses from the top of her head to her nose as if more clarity in her vision would help her make sense of it. "I suppose we could hem it but it's going to take a while." She knelt and adjusted the skirt and Abby almost keeled over on the riser.

Abby twisted the dress around her bust, biting her lower lip in frustration. "I think I like the other one better."

"But your fiancé is going to be blown away by this." Ella

unraveled a veil and propped herself on the riser, setting it on top of Abby's head. She spread the material on either side of her face like a set of a grandmother's curtains. She stepped back to review her work. "You are exquisite."

The fabric swished against everything it touched as she moved, crinolines catching on the interior layer. She could be heard coming for miles. Ella's pettiness started to fade when Abby blinked away tears.

"Would you like to take it off?" the seamstress asked.

Abby straightened her lopsided veil. "Yes, I would."

Ella was about to delay with another ludicrous suggestion, but the door opened, and a tall figure filled the doorway. She saw him in time to duck behind the shield of Abby's dress. Lincoln's quick steps stuttered to a halt. He obstructed any chance of Ella making a clean getaway.

Abby took in a sharp breath when he entered the room. "Lincoln! What are you doing here?"

Ella crawled toward the fitting room where she could watch their exchange in the mirror. Lincoln put his hand over his mouth as he took Abby in.

"What do you think?" Abby spread her arms, waddling in a circle to model it for him.

It was as if Ella could see Lincoln stringing together a diplomatic compliment. "I hate it," he whispered from behind his hand.

Abby brightened. "You do?"

Lincoln offered a smile. "It's the worst thing I've ever seen."

"It's an atrocity." Laughter spilled from Abby. "I took

someone's advice and didn't have the heart to tell her she was wrong."

The seamstress, who was leaned up against the doorway, cleared her throat. Ella put a finger to her lips and shushed her.

Lincoln took both Abby's hands in his. "We need to talk."

"About?" Abby asked, a slight waver in her voice.

Ella took out her phone to beg Jack for rescue and found all the calls and texts she'd missed. The most recent said, *I'm going on the ice. Triple axel or die trying.* Ella mouthed the words to herself, trying to decode his message.

She didn't have to, because an announcement rang out from the rink, cutting Lincoln off mid-sentence. It was enough to shatter the moment. She flattened herself to the floor and maneuvered to the periphery of the room. Lincoln and Abby peered out the window in the direction of the ice rink.

"Sweater guy?" Lincoln said, an amused grin on his face.

The others congregated near the window, giving Ella a few precious seconds to dart out of the store. She ran to the shelter of the rental area, hiding among the crowd. All the skaters cleared to the railings, shoppers stopping in their tracks as Jack geared up for the finale of his performance. He whipped around in a series of dizzying aerial turns and stuck the landing to uproarious applause.

He bowed in the center of the rink but kept his hands on his knees and wheezed. When he looked up, Ella snagged his eye. He waved at her as he got mobbed by skaters until she couldn't see him anymore.

Ella didn't want to interfere as he basked in the glow of their attention, resigning herself to a seating area to wait for him. He stood taller in his skates, buoyant with pride. His smile charmed her, even from this distance. Her cheeks chapped. Was she blushing?

A block away, Lincoln and Abby left the dress shop hand in hand. Ella deflated. All their efforts were a waste. The rejection went down slow and bitter. She wasn't going to stop what was already in motion, like defying gravity when in freefall.

Jack beckoned her onto the ice, and she lifted a finger to ask for one more minute. She rounded the corner where he couldn't see her. At the same time the tears she had been holding back came pouring out. There was an aching void where Lincoln had ripped out her heart. She didn't intend to hurt either of them, but to heap her anguish onto them to make them realize the mess they'd left behind. She longed to be seen, acknowledged. Maybe even get an apology. She knew better than to wish for things that wouldn't come to be.

Ella found a hidden corner away from the hubbub and sat on the snowy staircase. She put her head in her hands and gave herself permission to mourn her loss for the first time. The release was cathartic, like loosening a pressure valve inside her chest. Letting go of the expectations was the hardest part.

She shifted to the side when someone descended the steps behind her. The footsteps slowed, then became still. Ella wheeled around expecting Jack and instead found Mrs. Claus. The hopeful smile disappeared from her face.

"Are you here to lecture me?" Ella asked, pouting.

Mrs. Claus showed no hint of enjoyment in her appointed duties. She sat on the step above Ella's and draped her skirt over her knees. "I *did* warn you about the balance."

Tears flooded her eyes again. "I remember." She tugged her sleeves over her numb hands. "All I want to know is why it was so easy for him to walk away from me. Or why he hurt me without any regard to how he made me feel. He's going to go through with his wedding and leave me with nothing."

"We all make up stories in our heads about how things *should* be, but they're our version of the events. Life has too many variables for everything to work the way we think it will sometimes."

Ella had braced for a scathing retort, but Mrs. Claus' reply moved her. "Is your divorce what inspired you to help people like us?"

She gave Ella a soft smile. "I've seen it too many times to count. The holiday makes reason go out the window."

"I should get Jack and go back to the city. I've tortured him enough already today." She stood and brushed the snow from her jeans. "Thanks for not yelling at me."

"I don't yell. I inform." Mrs. Claus used the railing to help herself to her feet. "Now, if you'll excuse me, I'll be busy avoiding my ex-husband."

"How can you be so civil?"

She took a cigarette out from behind her ear. "Honey, when you've been around as many years as I have, you learn how to coexist."

Ella regained her composure and made her way back to the edge of the ice rink. Jack skated over to greet her and leaned into the ledge.

"Where have you been?" he said, his skin flushed and dotted with sweat. "I was looking everywhere for you. I thought you ditched me."

Ella didn't know whether to laugh or cry. "You were amazing out there. I had no idea you were such a good skater."

"Didn't know I had it in me." He kneaded the muscle in his thigh. "I may have pulled a hamstring."

"But you created the most spectacular diversion." She arched her hand through the air like a magician.

"I didn't think anyone would see me." His pleasant expression resonated in her, a snapshot from the past. She sorted her memories to place Jack there. It was like he belonged in every story of hers. She missed him already, and their trip wasn't over yet.

"I saw you," she said.

Jack's mouth settled into a line, not quite a smile, not quite a frown. "Is the wedding still on?"

The question was like getting a paper cut, sharp and small and causing a surprising amount of pain. "Unfortunately," Ella said.

Jack tilted his head to one side, and she knew their heartache was mutual. He put his hand closer to hers. "Grab some skates and come out on the ice with me. We have plenty of time before the wedding."

Ella propped on the railing to ease into Jack's orbit and inched her fingers forward until they touched his. "I'm not as good as you are."

He slotted his fingers between hers, and she was mesmerized by his touch. "I'll teach you."

She didn't want to let him go, but to slow everything down for a moment and revel in his company. She'd been guarded, shoving her attraction to him to the wayside with a million excuses for why she couldn't like him, but it was impossible to ignore how complete he made her feel.

"I should go get some skates," she said, running her thumb across the back of his hand.

"Mm-hmm," he said, eyes still on the place where their hands connected.

She unlaced her fingers from his and the buzz in her nerves propelled her forward. The rental stand was unattended, and she waited for someone to arrive to help her. Ella drummed the counter. Not a soul was around, the whole area deserted. After several awkward minutes waiting, she called out a hello.

Unwilling to pass up an opportunity to get close to Jack, she took a few steps toward the door hanging ajar behind the rental stand. "Is there someone back here?" she asked. She knocked, but there was no answer. "I'd like to rent some skates."

Ella nudged the door open with her knuckle and discovered an empty room. She ventured inside, knowing she was trespassing, puzzled by the starkness of the white walls. Again, she asked for help, but no one responded. Growing more annoyed, she passed into an adjoining room looking for an employee.

She reared back onto her heels and tried to make sense of her surroundings. The windowless room had a single desk in the center with a snoozing laptop on it. A bulletin board occupied the entire length of the wall, sheets of paper too numerous to count tacked onto it. It wasn't an office, or a breakroom, or having any discernible function. Ella checked behind her and traced her fingers over each sheet, pausing to read the individual profiles under the photos. Employees, perhaps. Each profile contained four pieces of information: a name, an occupation, a start date, and an expiry. The expiries were all within a range of the days surrounding the twenty-fifth of December.

She jerked her hand away when she touched the portrait of a familiar face. She removed the tack and held his sheet. The name under the photograph was Miles. But it was Jack's face staring back at her. Jack's smile. Jack's dimples. She flipped the page over to find a blank side.

Ella told herself to leave but was gripped with curiosity. She'd make sense of this error one way or another. She continued down the profiles, wondering what she'd accidentally stumbled upon, creasing the paper with the pressure of her hold. She slapped her hand over her open mouth when she discovered herself on the board. Under her picture was the name Christina.

"What *is* this?" she whispered.

Ella stole the sheet from the wall, folding it with the one with Jack's picture and stuffing it in her pocket. It was an ad campaign, she reasoned, giving credence to the expiration dates on all the profiles. They could be using their images and occupations to better define their customers.

The computer tempted her with the potential for more answers. Her feet and her better judgement drew her toward the door, but her stubborn mind craved more information. She dealt in facts and evidence, after all. Pausing to listen for anyone walking nearby, she brushed the mouse to wake the screen and clicked the single file on the desktop. It contained a list of names.

She knew this wasn't meant for her eyes, but she couldn't stop herself. The setting around them fueled her suspicions. From the hot cocoa at Snowfall Inn, to the all too helpful staff, to the general magical ambiance, there was something odd about the upstate, as if anyone who came here fell under its spell. She scrolled down the list and spotted her name. Ella read her profile. Again. And a third time. All the details matched, but that expiry date practically jumped off the screen.

When she found Jack's file, she swallowed a mouthful of fear. She found her nerve and opened it, her heart thudding, her head an inferno. Her eyes wandered over the screen, not wanting to attach to anything. Memories came to her, fast and blinding. She knew Jack, as if they'd already met. But when? How? She thought about social gatherings or community events where they might have intersected, but nothing was reachable.

Then, a terrible memory surfaced, like the shards of a nightmare. His face was framed by her hands. He'd looked her in the eyes and asked if it would hurt. She'd said no. She always said no. Then the image was gone.

She staggered backward. If she got to Jack, she would feel safe again. Normal.

As she ran out of the room, she crashed right into a teenage boy. He screamed. She screamed.

He grabbed her by both arms to steady her, eyes wide. "I'm sorry, miss, are you okay?"

Ella examined his freckled face trying to match it with any of the photos she'd seen on the wall. "I was… I needed…" What did she need? More than she could ask this brown-eyed boy for. "I wanted to rent some skates."

"I can help you with that." His smile was sincere and didn't cover for any nefarious intent.

Her thoughts were an unruly tangle as the young man assisted her with her skates. Would he believe her if she told him what she'd found? Would he laugh at her? She didn't trust her interpretation of the sheets of paper and the computer files. The evidence in her coat pocket would require further study.

She wobbled on the narrow blades like a fawn with its first steps, the railing firmly against her armpit as she clomped to the rink. After what she'd seen, it was a challenge to act natural and not wear her concern in her expression. There was no pressure in her life, not in a courtroom or a client meeting, comparable to Jack's watchful consideration as she slid onto the ice.

Winter Wonderland

Jack knew Ella would kill him if he told her how adorable he found her first timid step into the rink. He glided forward, thrusting an arm out to support her when her skate buckled. Her eyes remained fixed on the tips of her boots. He offered his hands for support and she accepted the invitation. Hers were warm and soft.

She moved her legs back and forth with quick, jerky motions in contrast to his long, graceful strides. Her nose wrinkled with her determination to get the form right. He didn't mind the slow pace to give his muscles a break from what he'd made them do. It was worth all the torn tendons to bail Ella out of her jam.

"You're getting it." He jiggled her arms. "Loosen up."

"I don't do that." She was more reserved than earlier in the day, her shoulders slumped and eyes downcast. He couldn't imagine the blow to her ego from seeing Lincoln and Abby in the same place. At least he had the benefit of half a world of distance.

"Too busy with work to relax." Without looking over his shoulder, he crossed his skates and floated effortlessly around the corner.

"You remembered what I said." Sadness tarnished her voice.

He grinned, hoping it would help revive her. "Hard to forget when you get asked by a total stranger to come to the upstate and crash her ex-boyfriend's wedding."

Ella severed her focus from the ice to meet his gaze. She pushed herself closer and matched his stride. "You're a sweet guy, Jack. I'm glad you're here."

"I am too."

Skaters zoomed past them. Ella crushed his knuckles as she grabbed him to keep from falling, but he was so enamored by her it didn't register. Her hands seemed made to fit his, and each time he touched her it set off a chain reaction of complicated emotions. Memories spun through his mind like a cut up movie reel with half the scenes missing. Each excerpt placed him in another time, but he couldn't make sense of it.

"What's next in your master plan?" he asked.

She gave him a halfhearted shrug.

"Nothing? You always have something cooked up."

She mumbled a response Jack had trouble hearing. He spun around so they were facing the same direction, keeping his hand linked with hers. He took himself out of his head, wholly present instead of badgering her with questions. The light wind breezed through his hair and cooled his scalp. Sunlight poured down from the cloudless sky. Ella was radiant in the corner of his eye, and he didn't know how to tell her that.

"I need a break from the shenanigans," she finally said.

"What would you like to do?"

"Be with you."

A nervous current cycled through him, an electric jolt to his system. For the first time all day he didn't care about the latest news from Delbravia or the rumors about who designed the gown and the cake. He didn't care that Prince What's-His-Face wrote his own vows or planned to whisk Piper away to a private estate on some obscure island in the Pacific for their honeymoon. What he did care about was Ella. She saw him when no one else did.

Her skates collided with his at the turn. A shriek pulled out of her throat, her arms windmills. Jack lunged forward and caught her, their chests coming together. He guided her into a vertical position, holding onto her longer than she needed him to.

He wiped his clammy palms on his pants. "You all right?"

Ella raked her fingers through her tousled hair. "I'm not usually this clumsy."

"That wasn't what I asked." He hoped smiling at her would break the impenetrable tension.

She repelled backward and her expression turned serious. "Jack, I…" She blinked up at him like she was trying to make sense of his existence.

He waved his hand in front of her face. "Hey. What's goin' on? You're acting funny."

Ella shook her head as if she'd temporarily left her body to be thrown back into it. She peeled her stare away and took a little of him with it. "I had the strangest deja-vu just now."

"About which part?"

A crease formed between her brows. He wished he knew the words to say to make it go away. "All of it. You, me, us."

Jack pressed his molars together. What he was feeling was something more than casual flirting. With her, it was easy, natural. It had been since they'd first started chatting at the bar, like an introduction wasn't necessary. "Have we met before? Because you're so familiar to me."

"I don't think so." She reached for her pocket, then let her arm drop at her side. The crease in her brow became more defined. "This day is going by too fast. I want to slow it down."

He looked at the sky. Clouds gathering on the horizon promised more snow. "We still have daylight left. Let's take advantage of it. Your choice."

"Do we really have a choice?"

He glanced around at the merriment, the performative happiness surrounding them on all sides. "Are you having an existential crisis?"

"No."

"Is it Lincoln?"

She filled her cheeks with air and blew them out. "No."

Jack almost told her what Lincoln had said in the jewelry store, how he knew what he'd done was problematic and premeditated. He placed himself in her position. Would it heal him to know Piper formed a relationship with the prince while Jack was just an obstacle she needed to get out of the way so they could be together? Unlikely. He'd spare Ella from the agony of the truth. Sometimes it was better to be blissfully unaware.

Butt out and hands forward, Ella maneuvered off the ice. He

went after her, cutting his blades into the surface for better traction.

"Wait, was it something I said? Or did?" His voice was strangled. "Can I fix it?"

"You didn't break anything that needs fixed. I need a minute, okay?" Ella shuffled off the ice, pried her skates from her feet, and dumped them on the counter.

He forced a breath that hung suspended in front of him. He leaned back into the railing and watched the skaters breeze by. A man attempted a spin and wiped out, rolling with laughter from his place on the ground. A memory played over top of his vision and yanked him outside the place where he stood. There was no beginning, no end either, and the details were faint. There was ice. There was blistering pain. And there was Ella.

Jack rubbed his eyes to buff it out. He was scrambling his experiences together. He skated to the opening and plopped down on a bench to remove his skates from his sweaty feet. He jumped when his phone vibrated against his side. When he read the name on the screen, he nearly dropped it onto the cement.

As if his fingers had lost all function, he weakened as he pressed the answer button. Piper's voice broke through bands of crackling static. "Can you hear me?" The desperation in his voice was pathetic. He pulled the phone away from his ear to protect it from a high-pitched drone, catching every third word. "Piper? Hello? I can't understand you."

He moved away from the ambient noise of the crowd only to get deafened by the unhappy wail of a child on Santa's lap. He plugged his other ear, straining to make sense of what she was saying. The line went dead. He called her back immediately. The call went straight to voicemail.

Jack stood frozen with disbelief that quickly eroded into a sinkhole of molten hot anger. In his mind's eye he saw himself hurling the phone as hard as he could and watching with sick satisfaction as it shattered into a billion shards of plastic.

He whipped around at a soft touch on his shoulder. Ella was there, blotting out the sunlight. She seemed to read his wide eyed expression.

"What happened?" she asked.

"Nothing," he lied, still clutching the phone in his fist.

"I'm sorry for the way I've been acting," she said, sliding her hand into her pocket. "It's been a trying day."

It took him a moment to reconfigure his brain to respond. "Would you like to go home? I'm sure there's a bus we can—"

"Horseback riding!" she declared, waving a glossy brochure at him. "We should go horseback riding."

Jack glanced at his watch. If they left now, he could catch a Christmas movie on TV and blank out to its hypnotizing electric glow. Anything to dull the pain in his chest. "If that's what you want."

"Yes, absolutely, no time to waste," she said.

Ella pulled him toward the car the same way she did through the den at the bed and breakfast. People gawked at them as they passed. He tried to join hands with her in a way that made it seem like he wasn't in a hostage situation.

Once on the road, Ella took the speed limit as a suggestion. He clutched the door handle at every turn, heart in his throat. At a four-way stop, she rapped her fingers on the steering wheel, hammering the rhythm of a song he knew but couldn't name. His whole day had gone that way, these misplaced memories zinging around his skull without a place to land.

She jerked the car into a spot in front of the stables, straddling the white line and not bothering to adjust the vehicle. Before he could utter a word, she was outside. He met her on the walk, sheepish and stewing with guilt.

Ella presented her palm. "Give me your phone."

He felt the color leave his face. Had she seen him debase himself at the rink at Piper's whim? He turned his hip away. "No. I need it."

She waggled her fingers. "If you have that phone, you're going to look at it every five seconds for a message from Piper, and I'm not letting you do that to yourself."

It was as if she'd asked him to extract a vital organ. "I won't look at it. I promise."

"You have been this whole time."

Sweat beaded under his collar at being caught this way. "Nuh-uh."

Ella lowered her chin and looked at him out of the tops of her eyes. "She's not going to call you and beg for forgiveness. If she cared about you at all, she wouldn't have treated you this way. It's over, Jack. Let it go."

The wound of being cast aside deepened. He longed to tell Ella how dirty and used up that phone call made him feel, how it defied all his expectations. Ella was right, and he hated it. "You didn't have to say it like that."

"I'm blunt. I'm sorry. I'm—" She swallowed hard. A fraction of a second passed as if she'd forgotten how to speak. "I'm a lawyer."

"Yeah, well, I'm a real person with real feelings," he snapped, louder than he meant to.

She bit her bottom lip between her teeth. As much as he could blame her for this, she wasn't at fault. All he wanted was for their argument to be over. Reframing his approach, he emptied his lungs of breath until the clutch of muscle released from his shoulders.

"I never thought it would end like this," he said.

Ella's eyes welled with an underlying sorrow he didn't understand. "The day isn't over yet."

He nodded. "You're right. I'm addicted to this thing and it's keeping me from enjoying our trip." He opened the car door and threw his phone in the console, then jogged to her side and revealed both hands. "No more distractions." She gave him a double high five at his decision.

A signature relieving the farm of any legal responsibility for injury and/or death was all that stood between them and the trail. Ella sat expertly alert in her saddle, while he braced himself every time the horse laid a hoof on uneven ground. Trust was difficult whenever something mismanaged it, be it human or animal or machine.

He knocked his knees into the mare's sides to catch up to Ella. Snow fell gracefully around them, sounds subdued under its weight, sparkling white decorating the branches and underbrush. Within the shelter of trees, it was only them.

"What's something you've always wanted to do?" Ella asked,

breaking the silence.

He thought for a moment, then said, "I want to write a book. There's this story in me that's dying to come out."

Ella's gaze shot toward the woods at the mournful hoot of an owl. "What's it about?"

His face heated like he'd been sunburned. "I don't know if I can explain it."

"Try," she pressed.

He'd never told anyone, even Piper, about his recurring dream. He recognized every part of it but woke before he could see it all the way through. He was warm and safe in the strange flickers of his subconscious. There was always someone else with him, but when his eyes flew open, he couldn't remember their face. He'd always believed if he wrote it down the second he could get his hands on a pen, he could mold it into something readable, but the images faded fast until they didn't exist at all.

"It's about love," he finally said, throat thick at his admission. "The kind you know with your whole self."

"A romance."

"Yeah. I believe a good love story can change the world."

She tossed her hair off her shoulder. "Even if it's about us misfits?"

"Even us." Regret squeezed his chest. That was a familiar feeling for him, the melancholy letdown of a season that was supposed to be joyful and merry and bright. "I know the whole story by heart, but I don't know how it ends."

"Happily ever after?" She grinned.

"Something like that."

Ella guided her horse into the clearing and gently tugged the reins. Snowcapped mountain slopes disappeared behind gray fog, extending for miles. It dwarfed them with its majesty. He drew the air into his lungs, disconnecting from the past, reconnecting to the future. They let the quiet gather. There was nothing important to say.

Jack's horse shifted under his saddle and rooted her nose in the snow. "I didn't ask you what you would do."

She smiled slightly. "I would show the people around me how much I care about them." She gave him a pointed look. "I owe you a huge debt for coming here with me. I'll try to make it up to you somehow."

Jack scratched a nonexistent itch on the side of his face. "You don't owe me anything. You've made my holiday a hundred percent better." He peeled back his sleeve and noted the time. It was falling away with reckless abandon. "It's getting late. Think we can actually keep this wedding from happening or do we accept defeat?"

Ella's tinkling laughter made it hard for him to look anywhere else. In her camelhair coat, she radiated against the monochrome backdrop. "You sure you're up for it?"

"I said I would, and here I am."

"Here you are," she said, the corners of her mouth falling.

They took the long way back to the stables, not saying much to each other. They bid farewell to their horses and returned to the car. The snow hadn't let up, covering their tire tracks and forcing Ella to forge a new path. Jack helped navigate through the endless white land, his phone a distant and unnecessary object he hadn't considered seeking.

On the way to Snowfall Inn, they detoured to a tailor where he was fitted for a suit. Ella insisted he wear a red bowtie, which he didn't admit to liking but did. She had an adventurous streak, coaxing him out of the places he felt secure, and it made him want to dive in without a stray thought of the consequences.

Next, they browsed a clothing store where every garment seemed to come in Ella's size. Even his suit tailoring had a certain level of perfection to it he couldn't quite grasp. This town and its elements were almost too orchestrated to be believed.

Ella slid the hangers one by one on the rail, selecting a dress, shoving it back. She grumbled to herself. "I don't know what will give off the right vibe."

He leaned his folded arms onto a four-way rack. "Something bold, like you." He detected a slight blush on her cheekbones at his compliment.

"Lincoln's family will be furious if I steal the spotlight from their beloved son. I can't wait." She lingered on a decision, then relented, hooking the hanger on the railing.

A pop of crimson attracted his eye. He brought the dress out from between its neighbors. "This. This is the one. Try it on."

Ella skimmed her fingers across the shiny fabric. Her lips curled into a coy smile. She bought the dress and a pair of matching heels, then tore off the tags and ducked into a fitting room, much to the objection of the shop clerk.

Jack paced the floor, hands in his pockets, bowtie slowly strangling him. A headache hinted at his temples. Sweat coated the small of his back. What did they keep the thermostat set at in this store, he wondered, a thousand degrees?

He quit pacing when Ella emerged. His heart lurched like it wanted to attach to hers. "Wow," he whispered.

She turned in a circle to model it for him. The dress hugged her form and accentuated her legs. Her swept up hair exposed the V-shaped back and long line of buttons. Her stiletto heels were a taunt: Ignore me. I dare you.

"What do you think?" she asked, jutting out a hip.

"You look…" None of the apt descriptors came to him. She was too beautiful for words. "Unforgettable."

Ella brushed her bangs from her face, suddenly bashful. "Let's make sure Lincoln never does." She donned her coat, hooked his arm, and away they went to the ceremony.

It's Beginning to Look A Lot Like Christmas

"Please tell me we shouldn't do this." Ella's hands were glued around the steering wheel as she stared into the creeping infiltration of night.

"We shouldn't do this," Jack said with all the confidence a man could muster.

She looked at him sideways. "You're not supposed to agree."

He turned his hands up with a shrug. "You told me to say it." He was impossibly dapper in his suit, and his playful innocence only made him more attractive.

Ella spied on the guests entering the chapel decked in their fineries. Lincoln's family had remained in town after the funeral to attend the wedding. That didn't seem coincidental. Making marriage a requirement for a business inheritance—specifically linking it to Christmas—was the strangest thing she'd come across in her career. Nothing about it added up. Coupling that with her odd discovery behind the skate rental, her mind was filled with conspiracies.

"Separating isn't working for us," she said, more out of fear than strategy. "No more divide and conquer. We're better when we're together."

"I agree." He polished his lapel with his knuckles. "I'll be your date *and* your accomplice."

For one fleeting moment, she considered putting the car in reverse and finding a private place where she could have Jack all to herself without these distractions. They could challenge the expiries and laugh about them later. She knew what was real. She was rational and precise. Fairy tales were for children. Thoughts centered, she stepped out of the car to face her next challenge, and after that they would be free to venture elsewhere.

Her feet were wet and numb by the time they got into the chapel. The heels she bought were ill-equipped for the deep snow, but their pointed tips made her look dangerous, like she brandished a weapon, so she had to have them. Jack tried to take her coat, but she insisted on keeping it within her reach in case she had to use it as a cover and flee. They found seats at the rear of the chapel where they could see the ceremony but stay off Lincoln's radar.

Jack draped his arm across the back of her seat. "I've never been to a wedding I wasn't invited to. It's like watching a football game with teams you don't root for. No investment."

"Oh, I'm invested." Ella pressed her cheek to Jack's shoulder when Lincoln's brother escorted their grandmother down the aisle. Jack's fingers flickered against his leg like he wanted them to be somewhere else. "There's definitely a loser in this game, and it isn't going to be me."

Her comment drew the attention of someone across the way. Jack clutched her a smidge closer when they recognized the woman at the same time. They snapped their gazes forward. Mrs. Claus crossed her arms and glared at them, and there was no misunderstanding the meaning of that silent warning. Ella wondered how much she knew, her mind spinning intricate theories until she gave herself a headache. She put her hand against the lining of her coat to be sure Mrs. Claus hadn't pickpocketed her on the way in. Jack's expiry date flashed across her mind and there wasn't anything she could do to forget what she knew.

Jack leaned into Ella and put his back to the Ghost of Christmas Regret. "There's something I didn't tell you," he said. Ella's stomach bottomed out. "She was in the room when I went back after the catering fiasco."

Ella tried to swallow past the jam in her throat, but it didn't relieve the constriction. Her job required years of careful practice never giving her vulnerabilities away. So, she deflected. "What did she say?"

"She told me to go home." He came close enough to kiss with a little forward motion. "But I didn't listen."

Before she could return the sentiment, Lincoln appeared at the end of the aisle to await his bride. Piano music swelled in the room and the guests quieted. Bridesmaids swathed in lavender floor-length dresses began the promenade. How they assembled this wedding in the short amount of time was a math problem Ella couldn't work out.

The melody changed, the officiant invited everyone to stand, and Abby came down the aisle. Ella rose and swooned over the scene. Weddings always got to her, no matter the couple or the circumstances. She had to admit, the dress was a better choice than the hideous thing she'd suggested, which would've made Abby look like an earthbound piñata.

Ella aligned herself with a tall man two rows up who blocked her view of the bride and groom uniting in matrimony. She didn't hear the opening remarks about love and togetherness. She was too preoccupied by Jack's fingers nudging their way between hers. They laced their hands together, a sign of solidarity. Out of the corner of her eye, she caught a glimpse of one of his dimples.

Next came the vows. The exchange of rings. Words and promises and lies all built on the broken foundation of her trust. Ella couldn't get enough air inside her chest. Her resolved drained down the back of her neck. The officiant uttered the line about speaking now or forever holding your peace.

Jack elbowed her in the ribs. "This is your moment."

Ella bunched the hem of her skirt. "I'm not objecting."

"Isn't that the whole reason we came here?"

"It's not legally binding. That only works in movies."

Jack scrutinized her with a sharp look of disapproval. "Then why go through all this torture if you don't have to?"

She untangled her fingers from his. He curled his empty hand into a loose fist in his lap. She missed his touch when it was gone but she wasn't going to be the first to budge to get it back.

His shoulders dropped. "Ella, I didn't mean to say that."

As the officiant asked them to seal their vows with a kiss she said, "That's my cue," and slunk from her seat and hurried down the aisle.

Her heels clacked the hardwood floor in the foyer, a screaming announcement of her presence. She found herself in the Subaru blowing lukewarm breaths into her cupped palms. She didn't rev the engine. The cold slowed her wild thoughts.

Ella pounded a fist on the steering wheel. She wanted to draw blood, leave an injury, cause Lincoln a scar to remember her by. She wanted to be real to him, a person who was valuable. A person whose heart could be broken.

Despite her pain and suffering, Lincoln was content, and nothing she did would change the course he was on. Urgency made her antsy in her seat. What a waste this was, coming here and facing off with a force she couldn't control. She wasn't killing time. Time was killing her.

Ella slipped the sheets of paper from her pocket. The text was stark and inflexible, and she rejected its pronouncement, cryptic as it was. She folded the sheets into smaller and smaller squares and reflected on Jack's entry into the bar. There was a single word in her head when he sat beside her: *Finally*. When she'd questioned the purpose of being here, it always came around to Jack. Ella was supposed to be here *because* of Jack. But why?

A rap on the window startled her and she lost all composure. She hid the sheets and unlocked the door. Jack brought a burst of frigid air into the car. She peered around him to be sure he wasn't being shadowed by their ever-present external conscience.

Jack stared at his knees like he couldn't believe they were attached to his body. "I shouldn't have said that."

"I needed to hear it," she said.

He turned his head and Ella noticed a marked difference in his eyes. They were tired and glassy, like he didn't have much left in the tank. It lit up an old corner of her memory. "Why *are* you doing this?" he asked.

Ella realized how rash her behaviors must have appeared to him. She dropped her chin to her chest. "Because I want to matter. I want to feel like someone cares about me."

"I do." He started to reach for her, then seemed to change his mind. "I think you're great."

Ella took the chance, grabbing his hand and holding it tight. "Why did you come here with me?"

"Because you asked. And because I wanted to." He skimmed his thumb over hers. "It's funny. Most of the time, people don't see me at all. But you did. It means a lot."

She considered showing him the papers she'd found and asking him to help her decipher its meaning. They could find a new place to channel their energies, another project to occupy them until Christmas was a crossed off date on the calendar. But if Ella was skilled at anything it was ruining important moments. Jack didn't deserve to be blindsided that way. She would tell him later, she decided, when her whipped up emotions had settled.

"Can I ask you something?" he said.

"Sure." Her heart pounded.

He took a breath. "Can you turn the car on? It's freezing in here."

Jarred by the unexpected question, she mangled a reply and revved the engine. Lincoln and Abby came bounding from the chapel, coated in that shiny "just married" sheen. He kissed her on the steps. And the walk. And all the way to the limo.

Ella relaxed the sneer plucking her upper lip. "Well, this is a disaster."

"It's not over. We *could* stop in for cake."

"I wasn't invited."

"I was." He flicked a brow and grinned, despite her roiling hesitation. "Come on, it'll be fun. I'll even throw in one dance for free."

She couldn't help but chuckle. "What do you usually charge?"

Jack touched his chest. "I'm a very hot commodity."

Ella almost lunged across the console and kissed him, but she tempered her desires and took the last leg of their journey back to Snowfall Inn. Blinding bands of snow made it hard to see, and it was difficult to believe something so soft could be so treacherous. Ella leaned closer to the windshield, steering out of skids and easing off the brake.

Something tugged at her more than the drive. It was Mrs. Claus warning her not to disrupt the balance. She feared the expiry predicted Jack's fate, possibly caused by an accident on the roadway in a place they were forbidden to come. Maybe he wouldn't live through the crash, and she would die tomorrow in a hospital with faded Christmas-themed window clings decorating the room of the intensive care unit. She blinked away the morbid vision before she obsessed over it further.

All her muscles released at once when they parked at the bed and breakfast. Her precious cargo was safe, at last.

The feeling didn't last long as they mingled with the guests in the cramped room. It was as if the entirety of the upstate had been invited to this soiree. They disguised themselves among them, and Ella was comforted by the persistent hum of conversation. Jack remained close and protective and she knew she could dive inside his embrace whenever she needed his shield.

Champagne flowed down Ella's throat and wrestled the tension from her body. The low lights and dressy white table linens created a romantic atmosphere. She would've loved it if the honorary couple was someone else. They loaded their plates with handcrafted hors d'oeuvres, delicate pastries and fancy cheeses.

"You've got to try this," Jack said with his mouth full as he pointed to the chocolate mousse pastry he'd taken a bite out of. "It might outrank the cocoa."

She hiccupped from the bubbles in her stomach. "Impossible."

He took it between his thumb and pointer finger and put it to her lips. His eyes fell to the side as if he'd acted without thinking. She eased forward and let him pop it in her mouth. She savored every bite, wishing it wouldn't end.

A commotion clattered through the room. Ella ducked behind Jack when the newlyweds made their entry. Jack applauded, and she scolded him for cheering for the opposing team. When Lincoln and Abby found their places at the head of the room, the best man called everyone to attention with a ding of his fork on the champagne flute. A hush fell over the room, and something came over Ella.

Lincoln's brother opened his mouth to give a speech, and Ella spoke first. "I'd like to make a toast."

Offended gasps cut the air. Heads rolled her direction and she instantly regretted her decision. The circle of guests repelled away from her like a drop of oil in water. Jack kept his eyes pinned open, begging her not to through his fixed smile. When Lincoln's pointed gaze landed on her, his face was transformed by anger, his phony mask ripped off for all to see.

"Ella? Why are you here?" His tone was dark, the muscle in his temple pulsating.

"She was in the dress shop earlier. She convinced me to put on that horrible gown." Abby twined her arms around Lincoln's waist. "Who are you?"

"Who am I?" Ella laughed despite the humorlessness of the situation. "Who am *I*? Tell her, Lincoln. Please share with everyone who I am."

Lincoln hadn't closed his gaping maw. He couldn't weasel out of it this time, not like yesterday. He glanced uncomfortably at his guests, then, as if he'd won, a smile split his face. "Abby, this is Ella. My family's lawyer."

The dismissal hit her in the navel like a sucker punch. All the time they'd spent together. The things they'd promised each other. Evaporating in three thoughtless words.

Abby's jaw dropped when she made the connection. "You said you were in fashion." She screwed her arms down. "No wonder you couldn't name a single designer."

A guffaw burst out of Lincoln's chest. "A fashion designer? Please."

"While we're on the subject of the truth, you should tell yours," Ella retorted. "Are you sure that's all I am to you, Lincoln? Your lawyer?"

He shook his head. "My *family's* lawyer."

"And your girlfriend."

Discord rumbled through the room. The horror moved in a wave from one end of the crowd to the other. Gazes shifted from Ella to Lincoln, who squirmed where he stood.

Abby stared up at Lincoln at the betrayal. "You didn't tell me you were seeing someone."

Lincoln caressed her cheek. "That's in the past now. It's over between us. I want to be with you."

Pressure built up in Ella's chest, so tight it could rupture. "I drove all the way here yesterday to find out you'd chosen someone else. You embarrassed me." Her voice wavered, and she restrained herself before she wept.

"You should go," Lincoln said. "You've done enough damage for one night."

"Hold on." Jack darted forward and threw himself between them. "Lincoln, you owe her an apology."

This time, everyone saw Jack.

"Sweater guy?" Lincoln exclaimed, his face reddening. He stuck his hand into the front of his wavy hair. "You were part of it too? I cannot believe this."

"My name is Jack, thank you very much." He tugged at the bottom of his jacket. "Ella deserves better than this. Better than you. You told me I would find someone to love on Christmas, and I have, but it's not the kind of love you assumed it was. Love is being present for someone, accepting them for who they are, and always giving them their dignity. The least you can do is say you're sorry for being such an asshole." He brought his lips together.

"Please," he added.

Ella waited a beat for Lincoln to fill the silence, for vindication. She knew then she was never getting her apology. Even if she did, it wouldn't heal the yawning hole in her heart.

She turned around and left the carnage behind her. Jack matched her pace and they absconded through the closest door, which led to the kitchen. Heart-shaped sugar cookies were laid out across serving platters. Rage possessed her. She smashed one to pieces and stuffed the remnants in her mouth.

Jack took a tentative step forward. "Ella." The way he said her name was doting and affectionate, but she wasn't inclined to stop.

"He couldn't even say sorry." She punished the rest of the tray, crumbling them to bits in her fists and leaving them as ugly and damaged as she felt on the inside.

His hand came over hers, firm and secure. "Ella."

She pounded the counter and cried the kind of soul cleansing sob that rips at the insides. She allowed herself to feel the sadness, the rejection, the humiliation.

Jack wiped the sticky frosting from her fingers with a dishtowel. The thoughtful gesture compelled her to throw her arms around his neck. He didn't hesitate like he had earlier, enveloping her completely. Overcome by his kindness, she held him and trembled.

"Are you cold?" he asked. "You can have my jacket."

"Don't take it off. It looks so good on you." She sniffled. "That was the nicest thing anyone has ever done for me."

He brought her head to his chest and stroked her hair. "I meant every word."

"Do you think I'm ridiculous?"

"Kind of. But I like that about you." He stood back, gaze dipping into hers. "Forget Lincoln. Forget all this. Let's have a proper Christmas together while we still can."

She dabbed her lashes, her makeup a total loss. "What do you mean by that?"

"Chop down a defenseless pine tree, hang stockings by the chimney with care, put out milk and cookies, the whole thing. All of it. Everything."

"Can we stay dressed up? I'd hate to waste a great outfit."

He pinched her chin. "Of course. And since every human in the upstate is on the other side of that wall, there's only one place to go."

She patted the part of her dress where pockets were sadly lacking. "I left the keys in my pocketbook. I can't go in there."

"I'll get it for you."

Ella watched Jack stride away and released a happy sigh. The clock on the wall read a quarter to eight. The night wasn't over yet. She resigned to stop fretting over the papers she'd found and enjoy the rest of her evening with him.

She put a broken cookie back together and mulled over what Jack said about love. She'd felt it too. Her heart fluttered when the door swung open. Ella pressed herself to the counter at the sight of the person standing there.

Mrs. Claus took her time plucking a cigarette out of her pack of Pall Malls. Ella's coat was looped over her arm. She rolled her cigarette between her fingers, a self-satisfied smile on her face. "What did I tell you?"

Ella's mouth didn't work. "Give me that."

She whipped the sheets out and shook them at her. "You don't know how much danger you've put yourself in. Jack too."

"Nothing happened. The balance is restored. Lincoln and Abby are married. You did your job." She forced out a huff. "I'm trying to do the right thing. Why do you keep ruining this for me?"

"It's for your own good. If you would listen for once in your life—"

Ella stomped her foot. "You don't know what's good for me. But I do. It's Jack. He respects me, and he's nice to me, and you're a chain-smoking stranger who won't leave me alone. Now please give me back my coat."

"Ready?" Jack called from the doorway. "Tick tock. Presents to buy and things to do. It's almost Christmas."

"Coming," she replied, snatching her coat and leaving Mrs. Claus in the wake of her unstoppable confidence.

"Who were you—"

Ella didn't let him finish, riffling around in her pocketbook. "Where are the keys?"

Jack grinned. "I traded them in for a new ride. Come see."

Last Christmas I Gave You My Heart

"Jack." Ella clucked her tongue at him. "I didn't think you had it in you."

"We need to move quick," he said, nudging her forward with a hand on the small of her back. He checked over his shoulder for anyone on their tail. "I paid a steep price for him to leave with us instead of Lincoln and Abby."

He and Ella dashed to where the horse drawn carriage was waiting. Jack helped her board. He'd already stashed the things they'd left in the car, so their departure wouldn't require another layover at the bed and breakfast. If they crossed paths with Lincoln again, they might get run out of town with pitchforks and torches.

They laughed as they hunkered down under a fleece throw, too small for two people and forcing them to snuggle together. The weather was no match for the Clydesdales faithfully trotting past places where cars were stuck in the drifts. A bottle of champagne rested in an ice bath at their feet. Jack popped the cork and sent it sailing into the dark. They took turns sipping straight from the source.

He wrapped an arm around her and rested his chin on her crown, relieved and untethered. To ensure there were no disruptions, he switched his phone off. There were much prettier things to admire when he didn't have his eyes down all the time.

A relentless headache intensified with the cold biting at his ears. He pressed the heel of his hand to his skull and massaged it in a circle.

"What's wrong?" Ella asked, staring at him intently.

"Too much champagne, not enough sleep," he replied. "*Somebody* woke me up early."

"Will this help?" Ella rummaged in her pocketbook and offered him a bottle of ibuprofen. He chased three pills with a swig of sparkling wine and apologized to his liver for his cruelty.

The chauffeur deposited them in a deserted lot in town. He was hesitant to stick around to take them to the bus stop until Jack sweetened the bribe with a hundred dollar bill. Jack's diaphragm seized as he stood, and he braced himself against the side of the carriage until it passed.

Ella stepped down wearing her boots instead of her heels. When she had two feet on the ground, she looked him over. "What's wrong?"

"Nothing." He gave her a thumbs up, smiling through the pain. Some walking around might help to shake off whatever ailed him.

"Promise?" There was an edge in her voice.

"Promise."

She wasn't convinced, face drawn with worry. He slipped his hand around hers, healed by her touch. They sauntered through the silent street, browsing the windows of shops that had closed early for the evening. The unhurried pace was something they couldn't replicate in the big city with its frenetic, always moving energy. Time seemed infinite under the canopy of stars.

"I wish we would've gone in some of these places," Ella said. "I don't think I can ever show my face in this town again, and I kind of like it here."

"I have a hunch," Jack said. He drifted away from Ella and tested the door handle of the toy store. It offered no resistance.

Ella peered at the opening. "This feels like a trap."

"It probably is."

"You get that feeling too?"

"The whole time we've been here." He remained outside the threshold, curiosity baiting him. Ella made him want to find trouble. "What's the penalty for breaking and entering?"

She tapped a finger against her lips, and he wondered what they might feel like against his. "Depends on the circumstances. Intent. Weapons possession. In some states it's a felony."

Jack shuffled backward through the door. "Oops. Don't tell anyone."

Ella rushed in behind him. "Now I'm an accessory to your crime." She swiped a cartoonish felt top hat from a rack and plopped it on her head. "At least put a disguise on."

He stretched the elastic band of a plastic superhero mask around his head and adjusted it so he could see. He couldn't tell if it was the darkness, or the fatigue, or the headache that forced him to squint to focus.

"Jack?" Ella said behind him.

"Yeah?" He spun around.

She dissolved into a fit of giggles, wearing away the seriousness of her expression. "My hero."

They spread through the store, jamming on mini keyboards and building a tower out of wooden blocks. She reenacted their encounter with Lincoln with puppets, throwing her voice when she said, "My name is Jack, thank you very much." He added a nagging Mrs. Claus into the act, making his puppet double over with a smoker's cough.

After losing five hands of Texas Hold-'Em, Jack grabbed a dart gun and sneaked away down an aisle. When Ella came searching for him, he jumped around the partition and fired until his stock was empty.

She squealed, hurling a foam ball at him. "This is war!" she cried.

He took cover behind a bookcase and removed his mask. He couldn't catch his breath, like he'd been shot into a higher elevation. His ribs constricted around his lungs. He cursed his body for malfunctioning when he needed it the most.

"Hey, look what I found," Ella said after she got sidetracked by an ornament display.

Jack tried to stand, but his knees stayed locked in a folded position. Panicked, he pried them straight again, hinging the joints until they loosened. Cramps moved in waves up his shins, his thighs. He sucked a gasp between his teeth he didn't want her to hear.

Ella found him on the floor with his legs splayed out like a broken marionette. "What happened?"

"I don't know." He rotated his feet in circles. "I may have overdone it on the ice. Kinda stiff."

She put the back of her hand to his forehead, testing for a fever. "You're a little pale. You feel okay?"

Jack loosened his bowtie. "I'll be fine."

"You'd tell me if you weren't, right?"

He nodded. It didn't convince her, her eyes still narrowed with concern.

She sat beside him, her finger threaded through an ornament hook. "I found one with your name on it."

"Thanks." He nudged his shoulder into hers.

"You're welcome." She returned the gesture.

Jack stashed the ornament in his breast pocket for safekeeping. They tidied the store and put everything where they'd found it. Ella left a wad of bills and a note on the counter stating they'd bought the ornament after hours. They invited themselves into a chocolate shop, where Ella broke a hunk of peanut butter fudge right off the display. She offered him a piece, but he declined at the behest of his uneasy stomach.

The vibrating sensation in his cells didn't wane, even in the fresh air. He couldn't identify the root of his symptoms, and they were a nuisance. It was like the flu and overexertion and a hangover wrapped in one unpleasant package.

Snow fluttered over the land again, and all was quiet and still. "I missed my favorite part of the wedding," Ella said, voice no more than a whisper.

"What's that?"

"The dancing."

"Let's dance, then." He escorted her to the gazebo and out of the snowfall.

She brushed the flakes from his coat. Her eyes glistened as she smiled up at him. "We don't have music."

"We don't need it." He wrapped his arm around her. She rested her cheek to his. He sang the opening lyrics of his favorite song to establish a beat they could sway with.

He forgot the rest of the words and hummed the melody instead. He twirled her around and drew her back, dipping her against the crook of his arm. Ella laced her fingers at the nape of his neck. He'd seen her pensive expression before. Not today. Not even yesterday. But from another time, another place.

"Do you ever get the sense you've known someone your whole life?" she asked as if she knew what he was thinking.

"Sometimes." He couldn't take his eyes off her, enraptured.

"Does it feel that way now?"

The gentle lights, the company, it was familiar as it was new. His heart raced. "It does."

Her eyes shifted to his mouth. "I want to kiss you."

Jack was struck with a pang of nervousness. "I would really like you to."

Their lips hovered close, almost touching. A sharp pain stabbed Jack through the middle, sudden and paralyzing. He clutched his belly and folded in half, the attack sending shockwaves through the rest of his trunk. His core flared with heat when he tried to straighten.

She held him steady, her hand firm against his chest. "Jack, you're on fire."

He mopped the perspiration from his hairline and held down the bile crawling up the back of his throat. "I need to lie down. I feel terrible."

Ella gripped his arm, digging in her fingernails. "You can't do that."

"I'm so sorry. I don't want this to end."

"You've probably had too much champagne. Let's go skiing, or sledding, or four wheeling, or some other snow-related activity to get the blood pumping."

Jack didn't have the strength to lift the corners of his mouth at his amusement of Ella's perpetual motion. "Maybe tomorrow after some rest."

"There is no tomorrow." Ella gasped at her own utterance.

"What are you talking about?" His vision doubled, then straightened.

Ella didn't blink. With great reluctance, she dug in her pocket and unfurled two pieces of paper, handing them to him. "I found these earlier. I didn't want to show you."

He closed one eye to better read text under his photograph, all of it meaningless. "How do they have my picture? And why does it have the wrong name?" He glanced up at her. "I don't understand."

"Look at the date." She pointed her finger into the crease, a deafening ricochet in his sensitive ear. He read the print at the end of her nail.

"I'm confused." His teeth rattled together with his

uncontrollable shivering. "What is this?"

Ella looked at him for a long time. "Do you remember your childhood? Where you're from? Where you went to school?"

It was impossible to think around the clattering in his brain. Information came in ambiguous fragments, the rest hidden behind a mental block he couldn't smash through. As hard as he dwelled on the past, nothing came to him, a big black void where his memories should be. He shook his head.

"What's your business called?" There was an uptick of urgency in her tone. "What street is it on? How many employees do you have?"

Kneading the crick in his side, he breathed between each constricting spasm. "I own and operate a small chain of grocery stores." He repeated the line like it had been programmed into him. "Wait…" He reread details on the paper, mind racing. "Where did you find this?" Trepidation squeezed his vocal cords.

"I'll show you."

He couldn't sort the assault on his senses as she led him to the employee area behind the skating rink. The overhead light singed the back of his eye sockets when she flicked it on. Printouts lined the wall, too many to count at a glance. Ella opened a file on a computer.

"Should we be doing this? I don't think we're supposed to—"

"Look." She clicked on a file titled "Jack." His roving gaze landed on the expiry date. Christmas Eve. This year.

"That's today," he said. "But…" Jack became very aware of his mortality at that moment. He undid the top button on his shirt.

"My expiry is tomorrow." She grabbed him by both arms and

could've snapped them in half they were so brittle. "Don't you understand? This has happened to us before, last Christmas, and the one before that. It'll happen again. It'll happen tonight."

He slithered out of her grasp, mouth dropped open in shock at her wild insinuation. "What are you talking about? I had a successful business, I was in love with Piper, and everything was fine. Everything. I know who I am, Ella."

She crowded him against the desk. "Have you seen summertime? Worn a t-shirt outside? Do you recall a time when it didn't snow, and it wasn't Christmas?"

His pulse thudded in his throat. "Stop it."

Her stare burned a hole through his eyes. "I knew you when you walked into the bar yesterday. I don't know how I knew, but I did. Can't you see? This is all a set-up. None of this is real."

"But it's real to me!" he cried. The loopy feeling washed over him again. The walls seemed closer than when they entered. "Mrs. Claus was right. I should never have come here. I should've stayed in the city."

Ella's bottom lip quivered. "You don't mean that."

"I need to go." He limped toward the door, legs wobbly.

"I'll take you home."

He restrained an agonized cry. "I'll find my own way."

"Jack!" she shouted. "You always leave first. My expiry is miserable without you."

Overcoming the deep ache in his bones, he turned. Ella's eyes were wide and wanting. Everything flashed white like he'd been hit upside the head. Whatever had been impeding his memory partially dissolved, providing a glimpse into something deeper.

A tear spilled down her cheek. "You remember me, don't you?"

"I do," he said, taking a step forward, "but I don't know why."

"Look harder." Ella interlaced her fingers and brought them to her heart, her plea resonating in the room. "Find me. Help me fill in all the blank spaces."

Jack shut his eyes and tunneled his way through his thoughts, reaching into the blackest depth. He saw fragments of their history on the insides of his eyelids, then his memories shifted into impeccable order. And all at once, clarity. There were no photos of him and Piper before mid-December because they didn't exist. He knew what love was because he'd lived it, over and over. He'd been drawn to that particular bar at that particular hour, despite every internal mechanism trying to reroute him.

His eyes fluttered open. His vision was fading, the colors less vibrant than before, but Ella was clear in the center of his gaze. His mind open to receive, he realized how the dream ended. With Ella. And without her too.

"We met last year," he said. "You were a radio DJ."

Her lips parted slightly at his revelation. "And you were a security guard."

Details emerged in short bursts. He envisioned the scenery, the wrap-around desk at the entrance where he'd first spoken to her as she came down the stairs in a huff. "And we were trying to stop—"

"—a media conglomerate from taking over the station!" they said in union.

Ella clapped and bounced on the balls of her feet. "That's it!" Her excitement subsided. "Did we succeed?"

Jack stared at his feet. "I don't think so."

"We're bad at this, aren't we?"

"Seems like it."

Ella wore that pinched expression of concern he'd seen her make a hundred times before. "I have all these memories of you and no context for them."

"It's like I've lived multiple lives and you're in all my stories." A sharp cramp hit him mercilessly in the side. He quaked from the pain. Ella threw her arms around him and held him upright. "Is this part of it too?"

"Every time." She nosed her way into the curve of his neck.

"What happens to me?"

She shook her head. "I can't tell you that."

"Please. I need to know."

"It's a lot like this. I'm completely helpless, and then you're gone."

"That means you have to endure this alone."

She nodded.

"No." He held her, every texture and slope as much a part of him as it was her. "I won't leave you. Not again."

Her arms came around his neck. She sobbed into his shoulder. "I don't want to lose you."

Jack separated from her and drew his fingertips across her shoulders, her arms, until he reached her hands. They'd stood like this in another life, resisting the inevitable. He knew the ending by heart.

He brushed the bridge of his nose over hers. "I don't want to forget the way I feel when I'm with you."

"What are we going to do?" She slipped her cold hands inside his, and he squeezed them tight.

The stiffness in his neck was unbearable as he looked up at the ceiling for some inspiration. The thing he saw there made him laugh and cry at the same time. Unable to collect himself in order to speak, he gestured at the mistletoe hanging above them.

Ella rested her forehead on his chest and laughed too. "I hate this place," she said.

He ran his knuckles along the edge of her jaw, memorizing every detail, committing it to memory. He wouldn't forget the way her eyes wrinkled at the corners when her smile was genuine, how she graced a room with her presence, how she never looked at anyone the way she looked at him. He'd cement it in the forefront of his mind, so it couldn't be stolen.

She lifted her chin. He molded his hands around her face. "Ella, I think I love you."

Pearly tears beaded her lashes. "I think I love you too." A smile broke free. "You better kiss me, because I'm not waiting until next year."

They caved into each other, closer and closer still, until his lips found hers. He wanted to pause there, linger forever in her touch, and never know what happened next.

He jerked with a start when someone behind them groaned. "I swear," a raspy voice said. "You two are going to be the death of me."

I'll Be Home for Christmas

Mrs. Claus let her hands slap against the sides of her legs. "Every year. Every damn year." She put herself between them and the door. They were trapped. "No matter what I do, where I put you, how many roadblocks I throw in your way, you always find each other. Every year you find each other."

Ella didn't release Jack for fear his skeleton would disintegrate without her support. Feverish heat billowed from his body. "We *have* met before," she said.

"Oh yes. Many times. As Allie and Josh, as Brian and Misty, as Brittany and Adam, as Mary and Andrew. I've done hard resets and I've mined out every bit of your memories and it never works." She stomped over to the computer and closed it, then began collecting the sheets from the wall. "You end up finding our command center—which you did in record time this year—and then I have to softly break the bad news to you while you stare at me and cry, just like you are right now. Then I restart you and you wake up and it's Christmas and we do it all over again."

Jack shifted his weight between his feet like his skin was too tight. "What are we?"

Her severe expression softened. "You're the last touchpoint everyone has before they find true love. Without you, their relationships never reach their full potential."

Ella pressed her hand against Jack's heart, reassured by its steady rhythm. "Why can't it be us?"

"Because it's not meant for you. You're invaluable to this process." Mrs. Claus's thin lips pursed at their predicament. "I try to stop you. I do. But you never listen."

Jack's breaths were labored. Ella knew she was losing him. Again. "How many times has this happened?" he asked.

Mrs. Claus crinkled her nose. "It's best if you don't know."

"How. Many. Times?" He was yelling now, a jarring fury burning in his eyes.

"Twenty-four." Mrs. Claus wrung her hands against her apron, like she was ridding herself of the knowledge of it.

His mouth went slack. "Excuse me? Twenty… four…" he didn't finish, his chest hitching with panicked breaths. "How do we not know? Why would you set us up this way?"

"I'm very sorry." Mrs. Claus tapped the stack of papers against the desk to even the edges. "If anything, you're persistent. I'll give you that. Foolish, but persistent."

Ella ran a soothing caress over Jack's arm to calm him. She couldn't remember everything, but she knew his condition worsened rapidly when he was upset. "We found each other twenty-four times. We'll do it again. It's the one thing we're good at."

"I don't want to do this again." Jack reached for the wall, putting his shoulder into it and wilting fast. His eyes were sunken and his color graying. He would succumb to his fate, leaving her to expire alone. She saw herself lying strewn out wherever she landed when the mourning became too great, waiting impatiently for the unavoidable.

Ella couldn't keep her composure any longer, the premonition of her distress making her froth with anger. "Are you just going to stand there and watch him suffer? Can't you do something?"

"I'm afraid it's not up to me," Mrs. Claus said.

"We didn't choose this!" Ella constricted her fear in her fists to keep herself contained—for both their sakes. "Why do you keep doing this to us?"

Mrs. Claus placed the sheets in a briefcase, paying little mind to her outburst. "Because you don't believe."

"In what?" Ella screamed.

Jack raised his hand like a child in class. "Can someone please call an ambulance?" He whimpered, then sank to the floor, collapsing into himself like a ribbon.

Ella dove forward, protecting his head from smacking the concrete. She unbuttoned his shirt and pulled his bowtie from under his collar. His lungs pumped erratically. He writhed and arched his spine, releasing a curdled wail. Ella shushed him, helpless and unable to provide any comfort beyond her presence.

He traced her cheek like he was imprinting it into his memory. "You've given me the best day of my life. Twenty-four best days."

"Don't do that." She wrapped his lifeless hand in hers. "Don't you dare start giving me a farewell address."

He groaned, a spasm lifting his knees. "Is this going to hurt?"

Teardrops fell all over her dress, darkening spots on the fabric. "Every time you ask me the same question, and every time I tell you no."

"Thanks for lying to me." He managed a weak smile.

She kissed Jack's forehead and kept her lips there, too frightened to look at anything else. If love was about giving people their dignity, then Jack deserved his. His entire body tremored, and she prayed for stillness.

"How does your story end?" she asked, eyelids pinched shut.

"It never ends," he whispered.

"How do you want it to end?"

"Not like this."

Ella opened her eyes. Suddenly everything was clear and crisp and in focus. "Then you need to change it." She lifted off him. "I finally understand. We have to believe in ourselves. In each other. I'm asking you to be brave if you trust me to get you somewhere safe."

"Is there time?" he asked.

She scrabbled for her phone. "Twenty minutes until midnight."

He rolled over until he was face-down, then craned his top half off the floor. Bringing his knees under him, he worked himself back until he was upright, head lolling. She ducked under his arm, and with a heave, hoisted him to his feet. She stumbled with every weaving step, maintaining a constant thrust of muscle and strength she didn't know she possessed.

They charged toward the carriage. Icy crystals of snow pelted every exposed part of her, stinging like pinpricks. The moonlight dimmed and brightened behind the intermittent clouds. Each step was a victory.

Partway to the carriage, Jack faltered. He went to his knees, gasping and wheezing.

"Keep going," she begged, tugging his arm.

He groaned, face twisted in a grimace. "I'm so tired. I don't want to disappoint you."

"We're almost there. We can do this."

Finding his inner reserves, he got up again. They pushed forward, the carriage in sight. His legs gave out mere inches from their destination. He landed in a snow drift, taking her down with him. Frigid snowballs fell under her neckline and melted down her front. The chauffeur tossed his magazine aside and leaped down to assist. Together they proffered Jack into the seat. She climbed inside, not a minute to spare.

"Drive," she said, swaddling Jack in the blanket, "as fast as you can toward the city."

"Ma'am, the roads are too dangerous," he objected. "They're practically impassible. Maybe we should take him to a hospital."

"I like that idea," Jack said.

"Please go!" she cried. The carriage pitched forward. The wheels creaked. And they were off.

Jack put his forehead in the crease of her neck, his breaths so shallow and slow she had to hold her hand near his mouth to feel them. She covered his head to block the unrelenting wind and rubbed his arms to stop the chill.

"Where would you go, if you could go anywhere?" she asked him, peering at the road, unable to discern it from the surrounding land. She wasn't even sure they were on it anymore.

His stubble prickled her chin when he smiled. "Hawaii."

"That sounds wonderful." Tears puddled up against her lashes, but she refused them. "Just imagine it. It'll be so warm. And sunny."

"I can wear a t-shirt outside." Despite their impending doom, he hadn't lost his humor.

"I can't wait to see you there someday." She couldn't deny the grief flooding through her at the possibility that she was wrong. She would find him, and they would break free, even if it took them twenty-four more tries to get it right.

They galloped past Snowfall Hill and the bus stop. The road snaked through the inky black forest and its eerie gnarled trees. A deafening crescendo of jingle bells hammered her ears. The smell of pine was so overwhelming she gagged. Snow limited visibility to a few inches. Two minutes to midnight, the final countdown.

Jack's eyes closed and didn't open again. "Merry Christmas, Ella."

"Merry Christmas, Jack."

A gray, stormy wall obstructed their path. The horses thundered forward, their whinnies echoing in the dark. She compressed him to her chest. She heard herself scream. A wave collapsed over the carriage, a suffocating avalanche of blinding white.

All I Want for Christmas is You

A gritty substance chafed Jack's cheek. He wiggled his fingers, his toes, as feeling returned to his extremities. He pried his head up and coughed out a mouthful of sand. It took a few seconds for him to get his faculties. A rhythmic whoosh carried on beyond where he lay sprawled out on his belly. The sun beat down on his back and cooked him inside his suit. Something hard and triangular dug into his ribs.

He scooped a handful of the beach into his palm and let the granules stream between his fingers. He sat upright, expecting a world of white. An expanse of boundless turquoise ocean extended before him. The prevailing wind swirled through his hair and clothes, the sky so clear and cloudless he could see the curvature of the earth on the horizon.

Jack's eyes fell to his hands. He turned his palms up. He touched his face. He was more himself than he'd ever been. Real.

Reinvigorated. He withdrew the object from his interior pocket, a Santa hat ornament with his name on it. He was having that dream again. The one where…

Memories came rushing in like the surf on the shore. Ella had given him the keepsake at the toy store. He'd danced with her. She'd carried him to his expiration in the back of a carriage. He remembered all of it, down to the liquid in his lungs and his stuttering heartbeat.

He sprung to his feet, muscles sore like they were after rigorous exercise. He tipped his head all the way back and spread his arms and screamed a celebratory cry. "Ella, I'm alive! I made it!" The only lifeform on the beach was a couple skittering crabs, and they were not impressed.

An unmistakable urge came over him to go and find her. It was what he'd heard right before he schlepped into a bar with the broken heart she helped repair. He knew she was there. He didn't know how he knew, but he did.

A magnetic pull drew him down the shoreline. He took his shoes off and stuffed his socks inside, then tied the laces together and slung them over his shoulder. The incoming tide lapped at his toes, a new and thrilling sensation. He rolled his pant legs a few turns and waded into the foamy sea.

He canvassed the breadth of a mile in search of her, but the buildings in the distance never seemed to get closer. Jack couldn't bear the heat, persistent and inescapable. By the time he reached any semblance of civilization, his shirt was soaked through with sweat, his jacket an anchor he dragged behind him.

A surfer waxing his board glanced up. He tossed his glossy

black shoulder-length hair back. "Aloha," he said.

"Hi." Jack couldn't assume a convincing pose that made him appear less alien.

The man gaped at him. "You look lost, dude. You fall off a cruise ship or something?"

Jack started to say, "A horse-drawn carriage," but knew that wouldn't help his case. "I'm looking for somebody."

He brushed off his hands and pointed to a bar in the distance. "Go there and ask for Sheila. Sheila knows everybody."

Jack nodded and sidestepped the man, then stopped and turned. "Can you tell me where I am?"

"Hawaii." He gave Jack a crooked smile and used his foot to pop his board nose up.

Jack barked a laugh. "No, seriously."

The man's eyes darted back and forth as if to say, "Can you believe this guy?" He shifted his weight between his feet, his tanned toes sinking into the sand. "Seriously."

"I did it. We did it. I'm in Hawaii." Jack pinched his shirt and tugged at it. "I'm wearing a t-shirt. Outside."

"That's... really cool, man. Good for you."

"Thank you." He shook the man's hand. His grip was loose around Jack's in his utter disbelief. "I'm going to find Ella while I can still remember."

More energized than he'd ever been, he jogged to the tiki bar offset from the sand. Palm trees were wrapped in lights, a sight he'd only seen in photographs. He imagined how disheveled he must've appeared in his undone suit and bare feet as he approached. He stripped down to his undershirt, then wandered to the bar, searching every face hoping to see hers.

"Something bothering you a drink might fix?" the bartender asked. She wore a pink tank top and denim shorts, not a stitch of holiday apparel to be seen, to his relief.

"I was told to ask for Sheila," he said.

She tapped her nametag. "That's me."

Jack attempted to string a few nouns and verbs together, but only managed to ask what day it was.

She looked past him like she was being pranked. "Christmas Day."

He knocked at the bar, unsure what to do next. "I told someone I'd find her, but I don't know where she is. Somebody said you know everyone."

Sheila polished a glass with a towel as if it helped her think. Jack couldn't keep his anxious fingers from twitching. "Wouldn't happen to be a woman wearing a red dress, would it?"

His spine shot straight. "Have you seen her?"

"Yeah, she came here looking for you." She gestured toward the beach. "She went that way."

"When?"

She shrugged. "A few minutes ago, maybe."

Jack didn't pause to thank her, using the divots in the sand to propel himself forward. He tore across the beach, dodging sunbathers and rainbow colored umbrellas and children building sandcastles. People milling about stared at him. They *saw* him. He was no longer invisible.

He spotted a figure wrapped in crimson in the distance staring wearily at the waves. He cupped his hands around his mouth.

"Ella!"

All motion ceased. Her hair levitated in the wind as she turned. "Jack!" she cried.

He ran. She ran. They met in the middle, falling into each other's arms. He lifted her from the ground and spun her around. There was no hesitation, nor care in his mind, and no mistletoe, when he leaned in and kissed her. A few of the beachgoers applauded. A few more huffed in disgust and told them to get a room.

She passed a shaking hand over his hair and face and chest. "You're okay."

"I feel great." He didn't know where to look, at her radiant skin, or the sunlight capturing the reddish strands of hair weaving through her dark brown mane, or the smile she reserved for him.

To his surprise, she shoved him backwards. "Why didn't you answer your phone? I've been calling and calling. I even called all your old iterations hoping you'd pick up."

Jack removed it from his pants pocket. It was still powered off. "Oops."

She slapped her forehead. "What am I going to do with you?"

He swept her hand into his and placed a kiss on the inside of her wrist. "Can you forgive me for that one?"

"This time."

"No more 'next times.' Only now. Today." He bit the inside of his lip to hold back the flood of emotions. "About last night."

Ella looked toward the ocean. "We don't have to talk about that."

He brought her close and the rest of the world fell away. "Last night I told you I thought I loved you, but I just do. I really, really do."

"I really, really do too."

Jack and Ella faced the ocean, traded a knowing grin, and sprinted for the water, letting the waves take them. They were average people who had done the extraordinary. They'd gotten their happily ever after, an ending Jack couldn't write more completely if he wanted to.

He took her around the waist, sundrenched and happy. "Merry Christmas, Ella."

She beamed. "Merry Christmas, Jack."

Acknowledgements

This story would not have been possible without the relentless love and support of my husband Jason, who has believed in this little writing dream of mine since the jump. I'm so thankful to you for always being my sounding board, my ideas guy, and the person who has never stopped believing in me.

I would like to thank my parents for bathing me in beautiful words since the day I was born. You taught me how to tell stories from an early age and gave me the space to paint pictures with words Also, to my brother, my imagination's co-pilot, my slapstick movie watching buddy. You fueled my love for satire and helped me polish my sarcasm skills. Thank you to my family and friends who have been there supporting me from the beginning.

Thanks to my critique partners and beta readers who devoted their time to helping me get this story to its final state. Holly, Allison, Willie, Courtney, Lily, Brittany, and Heather, I am in debt to you for all you've done to make this story shine.

Finally, to Bachelor Nation, my girls, who helped inspire this wild idea. I adore you.

Made in the USA
Lexington, KY
12 December 2019